MYSTERY HERD

There is big trouble on the Bates family's Owl ranch when Trinity reaches it. The foreman has been lynched and Vincent Battles has arrived to take his place, along with his rough crew. Cowhands are quitting and men are being shot at — Trinity included. And when Trinity manages to fit together the pieces of the puzzle of Owl's problems, the only solution his enemies can see is to try to kill him.

LOGAN WINTERS

MYSTERY HERD

Complete and Unabridged

LINFORD
Leicester

First published in Great Britain in 2012 by
Robert Hale Limited
London

First Linford Edition
published 2013
by arrangement with
Robert Hale Limited
London

A catalogue record for this book is available
from the British Library.

ISBN 978–1–4448–1745–4

Published by
F. A. Thorpe (Publishing)
Anstey, Leicestershire

Set by Words & Graphics Ltd.
Anstey, Leicestershire
Printed and bound in Great Britain by
T. J. International Ltd., Padstow, Cornwall

This book is printed on acid-free paper

1

It was an agreeable time and place. The horsemen had dismounted and loosened their saddle cinches to allow the horses to breathe easier as they grazed on the grass of the oak-stippled knoll. The long valley below them was rife with gold colored grass ready for mowing. A creek ran past prettily, appearing silver and purple in the slanting light of the downward tending sun. Far beyond the valley a ring of rugged, pine-stippled hills showed early shadows in their crevices. The breeze was fresh as it flowed across the knoll, rattling the leaves of the oak trees, but not cool enough to cause discomfort. It was Trinity's first visit to this south-eastern corner of Colorado Territory, and he liked what he was seeing.

Had it not been for the slowly swinging shadow the hanging man cast, it would have been a peaceful view.

Now Trinity again returned his attention to the lynched man whose tongue protruded and whose face was nearly black. He was a large man, Trinity noticed, with work hardened hands and a cowhand's clothes. His boots were missing.

His companion, Russell Bates, did not look at the dead man. He already knew who it was.

'His name is Dalton Remy — or that was his name,' young Russell Bates said, without turning to look at him or at Trinity. 'I don't know if a dead man is still entitled to a name.'

'That depends on what kind of man he was,' Trinity said. He removed his hat, ran his fingers through his reddish-brown hair and let the breeze finish arranging it before planting his Stetson once more.

'He was a good man,' Bates said, forcing himself to glance that way at the man who was no longer one of the living. 'He taught me a lot when I was a

2

kid — some that I didn't appreciate at the time.'

After they had tightened their cinches and again were aboard the horses, Bates went on, 'Remy was my father's foreman for years. He still was the last time I heard from Dad.'

Trinity nodded. He had already heard much of the story along the long trail. Russell's father had written him an urgent letter at Fort Bridger where he was serving out his enlistment in the cavalry. The old man had pleaded with Russell to come home. There was a dire emergency down on the Owl, which was the ranch's name and the quirky brand its livestock wore.

Since the Owl was also a provider of army beef, Russell had assumed his commander would grant him an emergency leave, but his request had been denied. Russell had taken matters into his own hands. One day while riding patrol, he had slipped away from his troop, put on the civilian clothing he had stashed in his saddle-bags, and headed off on his own. As he had asked Trinity:

'What was I to do? I have a duty to the army, but there's no duty stronger than that owed to one's family.'

He had met Trinity by chance while riding south, and it was a good thing he had. In his state of mind, in his haste, Bates hadn't even brought basic provisions along and he was half-starved before he encountered Trinity camped in the broken hills along the North Platte River. Trinity didn't talk much about himself, but he was a companionable man and when Bates told him his story, he agreed to ride along with him toward the Owl.

'Got nothing much else to do,' the tall man had told Bates. Trinity was willing to share his supplies and listen to Russell's speculation as they rode.

'My father didn't go into details in his letter — he was never much for writing,' Russell told him. 'He only said that someone was out to ruin the Owl, and I should get myself back home.

4

He's not young any more, Trinity. I could see by his squiggled writing that his hand was uncertain, trembling.'

'Who has been running the Owl since you've been gone?'

'Who? Dalton Remy,' Russell said, jerking his head toward the hanged man. 'He was foreman on the ranch for maybe twenty years, since Father drove the first herd up out of Texas. You see what's happened to him. I was worried before . . . now I'm plain scared.'

'Well,' Trinity said, trying to keep his voice level. 'It looks like we're nearly there.' Ahead through the scattering of oak trees he had spotted a collection of low buildings. 'I take it that's the Owl.'

'Yes,' Russell said. 'We've been on our land for the past hour.'

'We're almost there; your father will be able to tell you what the trouble is.'

'If he's . . . ' Russell's voice faded away. By now he had come to the conclusion that his father might be dead or dying, unable to speak.

'Who else is home who might be able

5

to tell you what's gone wrong?'

'My sisters. Holly and Millicent. Neither is likely to know much. I've never seen Millicent out on the range — she has no interest in where the money comes from, only in spending it,' Russell said without bitterness. 'As for Holly, she's so busy trying to prove she's mistress of the Owl that the cowhands duck for cover when they see her coming.'

'That's everybody?'

'I have an older brother, Earl, but he rode back to Texas a few years ago after he and my father got into some sort of squabble. We weren't close. He had a temper like Holly's. I didn't even know he was gone until a week had passed and one of the hands happened to mention it.'

Trinity only nodded in reply. They continued toward the yard of the house where a single blue spruce towered. Beyond the house a clump of barren cottonwood trees surrounded a red barn. There were six horses standing idle at the hitch rail, and a few men standing about, doing very little. For a working ranch, there was so little activity that it almost seemed a pall had fallen over the land.

'It's my father,' Russell said, his voice taut, throttled. 'He's dead. That must be what's happened.'

'Wait until you find out for sure,' Trinity said, but that did nothing to calm Russell Bates.

'If he were still alive and saw this many men standing idle, the world would be hearing about it.'

Trinity joined in silently adding their horses to those hitched to the rail, and followed Russell up on to the porch and through the door of the white house. The cowhands watched their passing without saying a word, expressionless eyes staring out from the shadows cast by the brims of their hats. Yes, Trinity thought, something was terribly wrong on the Owl.

Entering the living room where a low fire crackled and sent wavering flames

7

up the native stone chimney, they found a slender, elegantly attired young woman in deep purple velvet seated there, watching the fire.

'Russell,' she said, not with great surprise, nor in a welcoming tone, but merely acknowledging his presence. Trinity watched as she strode forward, took one of Russell's hands and studied him with her dark eyes. She was as tall as Russell Bates, perhaps an inch or so taller. Svelte and sleek, her black hair groomed and brushed to a shine which reflected the shifting firelight. 'How did you know?' she asked in a sultry, soft voice.

'It's true, then? Father's gone?'

'Not more than four hours ago.' She shifted her eyes to Trinity, a question behind them.

Russell, obviously shaken, was nevertheless alert enough to read the look and he said, 'Millicent, this is my friend, Trinity. Trinity, this is my sister, Millicent.'

The lady did not extend a hand and

so Trinity merely nodded. There was the patter of feet on the stairwell to their left and a youngish, red-haired girl in range clothes appeared. She paused halfway down the flight of steps and squinted at them.

'Russell? Just a little too late as always,' the girl said in a cutting voice. It wasn't the way Trinity would have liked to be welcomed to a family gathering. Russell, however, perhaps used to the tone, seemed to take the scolding in his stride.

'I got here as quickly as I could. Holly, this is my friend, Trinity.'

'What's he here for?' the redhead snapped and Trinity turned his eyes away to watch Millicent as she slinked back to her over-stuffed black leather chair and settled into it with feline grace. It was hard to believe that these two women were sisters who had shared the same upbringing.

'I want to go up and see Father,' Russell said, as Holly clumped down the stairs, her boot heels thudding heavily. She jammed her hands into the pockets of her faded jeans and looked up at her brother, her mouth tight.

'Well?' She nodded her head toward the stairs.

'First I wanted to ask you, have to ask you — what happened to Dalton Remy — if you know . . . '

'How would I know?' Holly Bates asked, tucking her hair into the gray Stetson she wore. 'The old man just came up missing two days ago. I guess he knew with Father gone there wouldn't be a place for him on the Owl any more.'

'That's not what happened!' Russell said, growing agitated. 'Besides, why wouldn't there be a place for him? He's been here since the first days. Father trusted him completely.'

'I can't say I did,' Holly said, her eyes smoldering. 'Besides, he was getting old. I brought in some younger blood to manage the ranch.'

'What do you mean?' a puzzled Russell Bates asked. Trinity was aware of the man standing in the shadows in front of an interior door, and he lowered his hand just slightly toward his holster.

'She means me,' the man said before strutting forward to join Holly Bates. He was tall and broad, his upper lip decorated with a black mustache, his blue eyes cold and impenetrable.

'Vincent Battles,' Russell said, obviously shocked by the man's appearance. 'My father told you once — '

'He's not around to tell me anything now, is he?' Battles asked coldly. 'Besides, Holly asked me to come up to help her. With your father gone, with Remy having drifted off, with you away in the army, she wanted someone who could manage things on the Owl.'

'That's right, Russ,' Holly said, her eyes fiercely challenging. 'We've got a big trail drive coming up, whether you know it or not. There's a lot of money involved — money the Owl needs. I can't manage the details and control all these cowhands by myself. Vincent was available — and he knows the Owl.'

Russell was silent for a long time, his mouth working with subdued emotion. There was obviously bad blood between him and Vincent Battles. 'I want to see Father,' he muttered finally and started past Holly and Battles toward the staircase. Trinity started to follow, but it was a private affair and he hadn't been invited. Battles and Holly had started toward the front door, a private conversation distracting them. That left Trinity alone with the oversized kitten, Millicent Bates, who continued to occupy the chair, watching the fire in silence. He took a seat close but not too near to her, crossing his legs, placing his hat on a knee.

'Have you known my brother long?' Millicent asked. Firelight swirled across the dark velvet of her dress, across her quite beautiful face.

'No, we just met along the trail,' Trinity replied.

'Oh, I see,' she said in a very soft voice that made Trinity lean nearer to hear her. 'So many new men around the place now — I don't know half of them.'

'There's always a lot of new hands hired around roundup time,' Trinity commented.

'Yes, but usually local boys: ones I've seen here and there or around town.'

'These aren't?' Trinity asked without expression.

'No, most of them seem to be from down in Texas. A few Mexican men as well. I guess Vincent must have brought them along.'

The way she said Vincent's name seemed to imply that she thought little of the man, unlike her sister, Holly. Trinity knew nothing of their past history, but it did occur to him that if Holly, in the absence of Dalton Remy, had decided to hire Vincent Battles as foreman, he had only done the reasonable thing in finding a new bunch of men to help with the long drive to Fort Bridger where the beeves were expected within the month.

The front door opened just as Trinity

glanced up to see Russell Bates making his heavy way down the stairs from his father's death bed. Holly came in the front door, a bounce in her steps just as Russell reached the foot of the stairs.

'Well?' Holly asked, snapping a riding quirt against her boot.

'Well what?' a doleful Russell asked.

'Well, Father's beyond talking to you, as you saw. Whatever he wanted to tell you, it's past thinking about now. There's no need for you to stay on at the Owl, Russ. Things are well in hand, with Vincent back.'

Russell Bates lifted his eyes. 'Are they?' he asked. 'I wonder.'

'They are — you'd be better off getting back to Fort Bridger before they court martial you and start organizing a firing squad.'

'I'm not worried about that — not just now,' Russell told his sister, although his drawn expression said otherwise.

'Well, do what you like,' Holly said carelessly. 'You know where your room is. But if your friend there' — she looked at Trinity — 'is going to be staying around, it'll have to be in the bunkhouse — and I expect to get some work out of him,' she finished with some heat before making her way to the inner part of the house.

'Sorry,' Russell mumbled to Trinity.

'No apology is necessary,' Trinity said. Millicent had remained curled up in her chair. Once or twice she glanced at the men as if she would say something, but she held her silence.

'Will you . . . do you mean to stay around for a while, Trinity?' Russell asked.

'I guess so, if I'm not putting anyone out. I could stand to catch some bunk time, rest my horse and maybe make a few dollars.'

'I'm glad,' Russell said, and the rush of relief in his voice was obvious. He was still a deeply troubled young man, perhaps more so now than ever.

Millicent uncoiled herself from chair and got to her feet. 'I believe I would like a cup of tea,' she said and then sort of glided away toward where Trinity figured the kitchen must be. She paused before reaching it, with her hand on the door, and turned her head toward Russell.

'You should know that Earl is on his way up from Texas.'

'Earl?' Aside he reminded Trinity, 'My older brother.'

'Of course, Earl. There's a lot still to be settled, isn't there? The reading of the will — we have to find out who has what coming. Who owns the Owl.'

'We'll all have a share, don't you think?'

'I don't know. In Father's family it was always the first-born son who inherited.'

'Earl has his own spread down in Texas,' Russell objected, but not strongly.

'I know,' Millicent answered, and she slipped away, passing through the doorway like a spirit.

'You've got yourself quite a mess, don't you?' Trinity said, approaching

16

Russell to stand in front of him. He looked down into the troubled boy's eyes.

'Yes. Yes, I do, Trinity. I'm glad that you're going to stay on here. I might need someone to talk to, to lean on for a little while.'

'I need a place to lay my head. My horse needs water and feed.'

'Yes, of course,' Russell said, grabbing his hat. 'I'll show you around and find you a cot in the bunkhouse. Let's get outside.'

Russell seemed to need to get out of the house, into the fresh air. Trinity knew why. He, too, could sense that there was more than the old man's death casting a heavy cloud over the house. There was something nebulous but quite evil at work here. Something threatening which hung over the Owl Ranch like a dark curse.

2

Russell Bates walked out of the house with Trinity into the bright sunlight. Although the sun was fading in the west, there was still enough of its light to strike the blue spruce tree in the yard and gild its tips. Gathering their horses, they started walking toward the stable with their mounts in tow. Bates would have to hide his bay horse, since it wore the tell-tale US brand, one brand even the running iron specialists stayed away from.

Trinity's black and white speckled pony wore the Rafter W brand out of Austin, Texas. That brand had been altered with differing success from time to time. A clumsy rustler running Double Diamond cattle had been hung over one such infraction. Outside the stable, Trinity got his first look at the Owl brand — the same mark their cattle would be wearing — on two saddle horses standing there.

The brand was merely a circle with two flaring iron loops within it that suggested rather than resembled an Owl. Trinity did not see how that brand could be tampered with successfully, though there was always a slick hand with a running iron or a hot cinch ring who would try to burn a new brand over anything that happened to come his way.

Russell saw Trinity studying the strange, quite distinctive brand. 'We had a smith here who was an artist in a small way — he came up with that iron for Father.'

'It's unusual,' Trinity commented.

'What do you think of my sisters?' Russell asked as they reached the hay- and manure-smelling building which was deep in shadow now, empty but for a few curious horses, their heads hanging over the lintel to their stalls, eyeing the entering men. 'And what do you think of Vincent Battles, Trinity?'

What the younger man was really

asking is what state the Owl seemed to be in and what he could do to take charge of affairs and prevent difficulties that his father had only alluded to in his last letter. There could be no answer to that. Trinity told him: 'I'd have to be around longer, to know those people better, to say, Russell.'

'I know,' Russell Bates said with a sigh as he slipped the saddle from his army bay and swung it over a partition. 'It's just that I don't like the feel of things around here. If Father were alive . . . '

But he wasn't. Russell who had come to the Owl to assist his father with some problem, now had no idea what the problem even was. It appeared there was some sort of secret game going on. Vincent Battles had been enlisted by Holly to come to her aid, they said. The man seemed to favor her. At any rate she had the right to ask for assistance with all that was happening. In response, perhaps, Millicent had written to her brother, Earl, asking for his help. Were they both trying to get ahead of the game before the elder Bates's will was read? Trinity couldn't even guess at this point, not after knowing them all for only a matter of minutes.

'Lewis Noble Bates was a man of stature, Trinity,' Russell said. 'My father was proud of his name, proud of the Owl, a good father to all of us. I have to discover what he was so troubled about that he wrote to me for help — even knowing that I was still on active duty with the army, that it might mean serious trouble for his son. I have to find out and tackle it.' As Russell said that, Trinity noticed the young man's hands tighten into fists. His determination to do his father's will was not feigned.

Trinity had whipped the striped saddle-blanket from the back of his spotted pony and was now brushing the animal. He asked: 'Did he leave any last communication for you?'

'None that I could find in his room. Either he didn't, was unable to . . . or someone took it.'

'That could only be one or the other of your sisters, couldn't it?'

'I didn't mean to make that sound as if I were accusing someone,' Russell said. 'I don't know that there ever was a last letter to me. He might have been too frail by that time to write. But,' he said, his voice rising, 'to answer your question, the only ones staying in the house are Holly, Millicent and our two servants: Alicia who does the cooking and cleaning, and her son Tonio, who helps her with the heavier household chores.'

'I don't see what we can do then, except keep our ears open and poke around a little,' Trinity said.

'You really are under no obligation to help me, Trinity,' Russell said.

'I don't mind,' he answered, putting his hand on Russell's shoulder. 'It's a sort of a puzzle, and I've always liked them. And I am reasonably good at solving them.'

'I thank you,' Russell said sincerely.

'Maybe things will come clear when Earl gets here — I don't know. In the meantime, let's get you settled in the bunkhouse. Holly was pretty clear about keeping you away from the big house. I don't know why.'

'It doesn't matter why. Not many people are comfortable about inviting a total stranger into their home.'

'No,' Russell agreed. 'It's funny, though — I am a stranger too now, even though I'm sharing a home with people I have known all my life.' He laughed, but the idea obviously did not amuse him.

Together they exited the stable as the lowering sun painted the upper reaches of the leafless cottonwood trees with a reddish light. Trinity shouldered his bedroll as they made their way toward the bunkhouse, where men were already drifting in from their day's work. Trinity could smell coffee boiling and beef frying. Smoke rose in an almost unruffled line from a black iron stove pipe to dissipate in the air.

'Cooky's at it. He burns a fairly good

steak,' Russell commented. 'At least you won't have to be living on trail grub for a while.'

There were hitch rails along the side of the bunkhouse, and the two men glanced at the many brands they wore. 'From Texas, mostly,' Trinity said. 'Rocking R. Hashmark. That one,' he said indicating a heavily muscled chestnut, 'is wearing a Poco Tia brand. That ranch is down near Juarez, Mexico.'

'I don't know much about that part of the country,' Russell said as a couple of cowboys walked past them. 'You know, Trinity, I hardly recognize a face I see. I used to know everyone that worked on the Owl.'

'Well, you've been gone for a few years.'

'Yes,' Russell said, 'but it's still an odd feeling — like coming home and not finding yourself at home.'

'Probably most of the men rode in with Vincent Battles.'

'I guess. He would have brought a

few extra men if he is supposed to be in charge of roundup and the cattle drive.'

'But . . . ' Trinity began, then halted, shaking his head.

'What, Trinity? What are you thinking?'

'Just that it's a hell of a long ride up to Colorado for these men with only the promise of a few months' work.'

'Maybe things are tough down south just now,' Russell suggested. 'A man has to ride where the work is.'

'I'll be seeing you in the morning,' Trinity said as they reached the front porch of the bunkhouse where a few idlers sat in wooden chairs, watching the sun begin to stain the western sky with a flourish of color.

'Want me to go in with you?' Russell offered.

'No. I'll just introduce myself around. It's probably better that way.'

'Whatever you say,' Russell agreed affably. 'Tomorrow morning, just look around and try to get a feel of the place. We'll put you to work the next day — that is if you're still planning to stay around for a while.'

'For a while,' Trinity said. Then he flashed a smile, one of only a few Russell Bates had seen on the tall man's face. Russell left Trinity on his own and stalked back toward the main house, his mind full of questions. Something was going on on the Owl, and he had no idea what it was. He was happy that he had at least one man he could trust on his side. Trinity was someone a man could count on.

The looks Trinity got from the men sitting on the porch were cool, appraising. They showed no animosity, but neither did they hold warmth. It wasn't unusual anywhere to be wary of a new man, but in Trinity's past experience cowboys had been happy enough to step up, introduce themselves, perhaps ask your name and where you were from. Nobody on the porch said a word to him as he passed by and entered the open door of the bunkhouse, carrying his Winchester and his bedroll.

At this end of the building, on his immediate left as he entered, was the cook's kitchen. After it, a long floor which formed a corridor between ranks of double-stacked wooden beds, ran through the bunkhouse to a back door. There was a high, narrow window every ten feet or so along each wall. They admitted little light at this hour. Trinity passed a trestle-table, an iron stove with split wood stacked in a crib beside it, more men with uncommunicative eyes and a few empty bunks with thin, rolled mattresses on them.

'I just got here,' he said in the direction of two men who were playing cards on an apple crate, positioned between two bunks. 'Any one of these beds with the rolled up mattress all right to take?'

'Take your choice,' said the man facing him, a dark haired, wiry cowboy with a nose that had been broken a few times. 'Anyone that doesn't like it can tell you about it later.'

Trinity supposed that was the best

invitation he was going to get, so he chose the lower bunk on the second rack from the rear door. He dropped his bedroll and spread the mattress flat, placing his rifle aside. Sitting for a minute, he removed his hat and studied his companions — those he could make out in the murk of falling darkness. No one he recognized — good. And no one who was likely to recognize him — better. If most of these men were up from south Texas, he was probably safe here. He had never worked down along the border.

Trinity had just smoothed out his blankets when an iron triangle started ringing. It was suppertime. The trestle-table was already crowded with hungry men by the time Trinity arrived. They apparently had a better sense of anticipation than he did.

A platter stacked with charcoal-dark steaks sat in the middle of the table. There was a bowl of potatoes roasted in an outside pit and bread and butter. Men rose, poked their forks into whatever they wanted and placed it on their plates. Coffee was in front of every seating. Only three or four men had removed their hats to eat, which was common — a man hated to be without his hat out here. Trinity paid attention to his meat and potatoes, not their faces but he did hear one round-faced, redheaded man say to the cook: 'Say Cooky, you got a lot of those chopped up chives on your potatoes, how come I got none of those?'

'Because I grow my own green onions,' the cook, a slope-shouldered, sharp-eyed man answered around a mouthful of steak. 'When you do the cooking here, you can have whatever you like; for now you'd just better like whatever you have.' The men at the table laughed. Another cowhand, a young man barely into his twenties spoke up: 'When I get rich I'm going to go somewhere where they don't know what a steak is.'

'I thought you liked beef, Bill.'

'Every day?'

'That's about all that grows on the Owl,' the second cowhand answered.

'Nah,' a third interjected, 'we've got a good crop of hay this year, Bill.'

'I guess your choice is steaks or grazing,' a third man said.

Across the table from Trinity, an older man with a sun-wrinkled face and a grizzled beard looked up and asked, 'Who all's going up to Dos Picos with me tomorrow?'

'I'll be along,' the younger man called Bill answered. A few others around the table said they would also be riding with him.

'I hate looking for strays up there,' the older man grumbled. 'In that tangle of brush and canyons! I never have figured out if the cows were smart enough to hide up there so they wouldn't have to go along on roundup, or just too stupid to find their way out.'

'We'll help 'em find their way,' Bill said

'I lost two good ponies up there last year — both with a broken leg.

Damned Dos Picos!'

'How about you, stranger?' one of them asked, and Trinity saw the eyes of the redheaded man on him. 'Are you going up there with us?'

'No,' Trinity answered evenly, cutting another piece of meat from his steak. 'Not tomorrow, at least. The boss told me just to look around and get a feel for the place.'

'Vincent Battles told you that?' another man scoffed.

'No, not Battles. I was hired on by Russell Bates. I take my orders from him.'

'I heard the squirt was back,' the redhead said. No one raised a voice to reply, but there was a muffled, discontented murmur that passed around the table. It was obvious that these men were all loyal to Battles, followed only his instructions and would disregard any orders Russell Bates would issue.

'Have fun, then,' someone grumbled. 'The rest of us have to work to earn our pay.' He rose, slapped down knife and

31

fork and stalked to his bunk. Trinity figured supper was over. He rose and walked to his own bed where he stretched out, hands behind his head, and listened to the sounds of the cowboys preparing for bed, swapping stories, playing cards.

A shadow fell across him, blocking the lantern light from his eyes, and he looked up. He had seen the man who now stood over him earlier. Dark-haired, wiry with a nose that had seen some trouble in its time.

'I want you up and out of that bed,' the stranger said.

'Leave him alone, Willie,' someone shouted. 'He's got to rest up to do nothing tomorrow!'

A small group of cowboys were beginning to gather to watch the exchange. A few of them wore broad smiles.

'You're the one who told me to choose any bunk I liked,' Trinity said, swinging his feet to the floor.

'Yeah, and if you remember, I also

told you that anyone who didn't like it could tell you later. Well, I'm telling you now: I don't like it. I've been saving that bunk for a friend of mine; he just rode in.'

'All right,' Trinity said, getting to his feet. 'I don't mind moving.' Not enough to start a fight on his first day on the Owl Ranch. He began removing his blankets. 'What about that next one up? Is that all right with you?'

'No, it's not,' the man named Willie said, stepping near. He smiled, showing two broken teeth. My friend seems to have brought another friend along with him. They kind of like bunking side by side.'

'I see,' Trinity answered. It was obvious that Willie was enjoying this. His face was illuminated with a sort of dark glee. 'I'm not particular, which bunk can I take then?'

'I've got a lot of friends coming,' Willie said, barely containing a snicker. Trinity saw that the man's fists were bunched now. 'All the bunks are going

33

to be pretty well filled. Why don't you just take your blankets outside and watch the stars while you fall asleep. The nights haven't been that cold, and there's a soft piece of ground over near the hog pen. It might not smell the best . . .'

'But you're saying it would smell better than it does here,' Trinity said coldly and Willie, seeing the hard look in Trinity's cold gray eyes seemed to be realizing for the first time that he might have gone too far. But men like that don't back down; they can't afford to when, as now, they had a gathered crowd to watch the bullying.

'I didn't like that remark,' Willie managed to snarl, regaining his aggressive attitude temporarily.

'You weren't supposed to,' Trinity said, dropping his blankets back on the bunk. 'I'm tired of you, friend. Why don't you go away and let me get some rest?'

Willie was a few inches shorter than Trinity, and weighed at least ten

pounds less, some of it poorly distrib-
uted. Nevertheless, he pushed ahead,
glancing at the men who were now
grouped more closely around them.

'There's a lot of men here,' Willie
tried.

'Yes,' Trinity agreed, 'but I don't have
to fight them all. I figure once I break
you up some, things will settle down.'

'Why you couldn't — ' Willie didn't
finish his sentence; he hadn't intended
to. With his face now flushed with fury,
he swung a wild right hand at Trinity's
head. Trinity managed to draw aside a
few inches and Willie's blow landed
painfully, but harmlessly, on Trinity's
ear. Beyond Willie, Trinity could see the
excited faces of the crew now crowding
ever closer, cheering Willie on.

Trinity raised both fists and sent a
jolting straight left jab into Willie's face.
The belligerent cowboy staggered back
a few steps, coming up against the
neighboring double bunk bed.

'Why you bastard,' Willie growled as
if taking offense that someone would

35

fight back. He tilted his head back, took a deep breath and lunged forward, wind-milling lefts and rights at Trinity, striking the top of his skull and his shoulders. There was more rage than muscle behind the blows.

The two men had turned during the exchange. Trinity now faced the back door of the bunkhouse. A panting, hunched-forward Willie stood in front of him. The broken-nosed man drove his body against Trinity's, his shoulder meeting Trinity's chest solidly and Trinity was driven roughly backward. Grinning faces swam past his vision. The cowhands continued to cheer Willie's efforts. Unable to stop the rush, Trinity's leather soled boots slid across the aisle of the bunk-house until he was brought up sharply.

He hit the iron standing stove violently, the metal slamming into his back just above his belt line, and he felt his kidneys jolt free. The pain was stunning. Trinity gasped for breath, tried to fight back the hurt. Willie had his man where he wanted him and now he stretched

36

out his stubby, powerful hands and grabbed Trinity by the throat, trying to throttle him.

The pain swirled in Trinity's head, lighting a small fireworks display behind his eyes. He was alert enough, however, to bring his arms up inside of Willie's and slam them outward, breaking the wild-eyed man's grip. Willie took one step back and Trinity struck down with his forearm, driving it into Willie's nose. Blood spewed from it and Willie bent down in a protective reflex. Trinity's knee drove up and slammed into Willie's face. If Willie's nose had not been broken by the forearm smash, it definitely was now.

Willie lifted his fists as if to continue the fight, but he didn't have it in him. Trinity swung a jolting uppercut into his adversary's blood-smeared face and Willie's eyes rolled back, the intelligence battered out of them. Willie went to his knees and then slumped forward on to his face to lie against the wooden floor.

The men gathered around them were silent now. Trinity let his gaze sweep over them, not knowing what their intentions might be now. Then, pushing a few men aside, he staggered to his bunk and lay down to try to ease the demanding ache in his lower back.

It was a while before Willie was carried back to his bunk and the bunkhouse lanterns were turned down. Then Trinity lay awake and alone in the long depths of the building, listening to a few men whisper, cough, mutter, then pull their blankets up to fall into communal sleep. He watched the sliver of a yellow moon rising beyond the high window opposite his bunk. He heard frogs grumping outside somewhere. The pain in his back seemed to ease a little as the hours passed and he finally fell into an uncomfortable sleep, his Colt revolver in his hand beneath the blankets, ending his first day on the Owl Ranch.

3

The pale red glow of coming dawn could be seen through the window when Trinity next opened his eyes, and he rose quickly — though he was brought up short by a stab of pain in his back; he had definitely had a kidney jolted loose of its moorings. He pulled up his boots, keeping an eye on the still forms of the sleeping men around him. He didn't know what sort of reception he could expect on this morning, but he wanted to be the first one out of the bunkhouse to solve any possible problems.

As he walked toward the front door, carrying his Winchester, he smelled coffee boiling and bacon being fried. He went into the kitchen where the cook was busy slicing thick strips from a side of bacon. Two black cast iron skillets already sizzled on the stove, loaded with bacon. Three or four dozen eggs, mostly white-shelled, filled a ceramic bowl. The cook glanced up without much apparent interest.

'You're early,' Cooky said. 'Come when you hear the triangle ringing.'

'I won't be staying for breakfast. I just wanted to see if I could snag a cup of coffee.'

'Help yourself — it should be boiled by now. Boys gave you a pretty rough time of it last night, didn't they?'

'I don't mind a little razzing,' Trinity said, pouring coffee into a tin cup he had found, 'being a new man here. But that went a little beyond hazing. Willie was trying to do some real damage.'

'That's just Willie,' Cooky said without apparent sympathy. 'I hope you're not going to let him drive you off. Not if you need a job.'

'He's not,' Trinity said. 'I don't need the job, but I've hired on to do it.'

Cooky glanced at him again, the comment making little sense to him. He shrugged, turned the bacon with a long-handled fork and said, 'I'll be serving it up in a few minutes.'

Trinity finished the cup of hot, strong, bitter coffee and put his cup down. 'I'm going out now. I don't much feel like seeing anybody this morning.'

The cook frowned and nodded his understanding. He inclined his head toward a straw basket covered with a cloth. 'Grab yourself a couple of biscuits to take along.'

'Thanks, I will,' Trinity answered and he lifted two of the still-warm biscuits and placed them in his coat pocket. 'I'll be seeing you,' he said to the cook. Trinity had heard the sounds of men stirring and decided it was time to make his exit.

The outside air struck him coldly. Thin rime glossed the land, colored now by the pre-dawn light of the sun. Squinting toward the west he could just make out the thrusting bulk of the Colorado Rockies. All around the ranch low, tortured, broken hills encircled the valley, crowding in on it. He knew a river ran across the land somewhere nearby, but he could not see any sign of it.

Trinity started toward the stable. Flocks of small birds fluttered and chittered madly in the barren cotton-wood grove.

No one was at work in the stable yet, which suited Trinity. His piebald horse looked up with apparent eagerness. There was ice on his chin whiskers. Trinity saw that the oat bin had been nearly emptied. The horse had eaten well overnight.

Saddling and slipping the piebald its bit, Trinity considered what he had seen so far on the Owl. The owner of the ranch, Lewis Noble Bates had died, gone before he could tell his son what was so important that he urged him to come home even though he was enlisted in the army. The elder Bates must have known what sort of situation that would put Russell in, so it must have been something dire. But what?

The Owl foreman, Dalton Remy, had

been hanged — because he knew too much? Who had done that killing? A new foreman had been brought in immediately or sent for prior to Remy's death, apparently by Holly Bates. Vincent Battles had arrived with lots of presumably hand-picked men. The older sister, Millicent, seemed unaware of anything that was happening on the Owl, or was simply unconcerned about matters.

Trinity himself had been assaulted violently last night. Simply because he rode with Russell Bates? To top that the older brother, Earl Bates, was due to arrive from Texas, perhaps looking to inherit the Owl.

Altogether things seemed to make no coherent pattern, no sense. But Trinity knew there was a pattern there — one of deceit stitched together with threads of violence. If he could only find one loose thread and start tugging at it . . .

'What do you want?' the querulous demand came from the shadows of the stable Trinity had taken to be empty.

The voice belonged to a Spanish-looking kid of fifteen or sixteen. He stood glowering at Trinity over a stall partition.

'I came for my horse,' Trinity said. 'The spotted black horse.'

'The one wearing a Rafter W brand.'

'That's right. You're pretty observant,' Trinity said as he slung his saddle from the partition where he had left it.

'I know all about horses,' the kid said, slipping from the stall to face Trinity. He was tall, but still had a boy's spindly arms. 'I seen that bay horse there and I knew it was army stock from its US brand. I figured out that Russell Bates was back before anyone told me.'

'You can learn a lot studying brands,' Trinity commented, smoothing the striped blanket on his horse's back.

'You came with Russell — are you an army officer?'

'Why do you ask that?'

'I wanted to find out. I know enlisted men all ride bay horses, but officers are allowed to provide their own.'

'You know quite a bit.'

'Yes. The last army officer who came here explained it to me. He was riding a white horse with a gray mane and tail.'

'Was he?' Trinity asked, positioning his saddle.

'Yes, that's how I learn about these things, hanging around the stable. I like horses more than anything. I sure like being around the stable better than what I'm doing now — I even clean up the stalls for free sometimes when Roger has had a rough night with his whiskey.'

'Roger's the stable man?'

'Supposed to be, but he's getting old and kind of dry inside. I figure I might be able to get his job some day.'

'Your name must be Tonio,' Trinity said.

'How'd you guess that?' the boy asked in astonishment.

'Not from reading your brand. Russell told me about you and your mother.'

'He did?' Tonio asked with a flush of pride. 'That I am good with horses?'

'He only said that you are Alicia's son

45

and that you help her.'

Almost as if that were her cue, a Spanish woman with wide dark eyes, in her mid-thirties, entered the stable. The brilliant new sunlight behind her showed a woman of middle height, with fine features only slightly blurred by the onset of middle age, wearing a striped skirt and a white blouse. Her hair was piled on top of her head, held in place by a Spanish comb.

'Tonio!' she said. 'I need you in the kitchen now. Come and set the places for breakfast.'

'I'm coming,' Tonio answered. There was a hint of childish rebellion in his voice, but he smiled shyly at Trinity, brushed his hand along the piebald's sleek neck and went out.

'We'd better be going too,' Trinity told the horse as he slipped his long gun into its saddle scabbard. There was no point in waiting around to see if someone wanted to start a confrontation.

Trinity's kidney's complained as he

swung into the saddle. From experience he knew this would be a lingering pain, flaring up with every sudden movement. Sunlight was bright through the skeletal branches of the cottonwoods and rich and golden where it struck the upper reaches of the lone blue spruce. Men were moving around near the bunkhouse, gathering on the porch to smoke, but Trinity paid them no mind as he swung his horse westward, away from the glare of the rising sun, and headed out on to the long-grass flats. There was a scattering of prairie flowers: blue gentian, star flowers and purple lupines, and fields of yellow and white mustard.

There were also healthy clumps of live oak trees, their prickly little leaves remaining green no matter what the time of year. The air was still and crystalline. To the north a few thin pennant-shaped clouds drifted eastward. There were yammering crows in the grass and a pair of golden eagles soaring far above them. Trinity smiled to himself — to think he was being paid for this sort of work!

For no particular reason he decided to swing southward. He rode easily, the sun warming him, the horse moving easily beneath him. Several times the horse's hoofs startled pheasant from the long grass which took off with wing beats.

Trinity drew up with a frown. In the shade of a half dozen jack pines on a low knoll to his right, a lone horseman was watching his approach. Trinity had loosened his Winchester in its scabbard before he saw that the lone horseman had lifted a hand and was waving him in that direction. Warily he turned the piebald's head that way.

He was within fifty yards or so before he recognized the rider in blue jeans, red-checked shirt and fawn-colored Stetson hat as Holly Bates. She sat on a perky-looking little paint pony.

'Good morning,' Trinity said as he reined up beside her. Holly's face was not so set, her eyes not so hard as when he had met her the day before. Perhaps,

Trinity considered, he had just happened to meet her on a very bad day, the day her father died.

''Morning,' Holly answered A slight breeze had risen and it toyed with a few wisps of red hair that had fallen free of the Stetson's confines.

'You're out early,' he said.

'Well, I just felt like a ride. How about you?'

'I wanted to do what Russell suggested — get a look at the land, the ranch.'

'I'm getting a little hungry,' Holly told him. 'I shouldn't have ridden out without eating, but Alicia was serving up some of her Mexican grub this morning. I like eggs well enough, but I like to be able to see them, not have them all smothered in hot sauce and onions.' She studied his face. 'You didn't eat either, did you?'

'No.' Trinity reached into his coat pocket and pulled out one of the biscuits he had been saving. 'But I have two of these. I'm willing to share.'

Holly smiled, not unprettily, and took the biscuit. 'Is this how Cooky is sending the men out these days.'

'No, but I was up early. It didn't seem like a good morning to linger over breakfast.' He went on to tell her sketchily what had happened to him the night before.

'That would have been Willie Meese.'

'We never got properly introduced,' Trinity said.

'He has a habit of hazing the new men, the young ones. Nailing their boots to the floor, hiding their blankets.'

'This was a little more than that,' Trinity said, shifting in the saddle for his kidneys' sake.

'Yes, I can see it was,' Holly replied, eyeing Trinity's face. Without a mirror he couldn't tell, but he must have gotten marked up some in the fight, judging from her expression. 'Well,' Holly said, washing down her biscuit with a drink from her canteen, 'we can't sit here all day — how would you like a guided tour?'

50

'That suits me, if you have the time.'

'I've given myself the day off,' she said. 'I figure Russell and Vince Battles will be at odds all day, and my only other choice was to sit home with my sister — I swear Millicent is going to grow roots in that chair of hers.'

'I'd always thought that a couple of women would be happy to share a conversation outside of the hearing of men.'

'Millicent doesn't talk to me,' Holly said with asperity.

Trinity didn't comment, but his thought was that maybe this was simply a case of the sisters having different interests. Millicent cared about her home, about fashion and leisure while Holly was a horse-woman, one who liked the outdoors, long grass and wind.

'Want to look the herd over?' Holly asked, answering Trinity's desire without his having to ask. 'If you look hard through the mist in the valley,' she said, pointing that way, 'you can see where they're gathered.'

Looking that way, Trinity could indeed see a herd of about five-hundred Owl cattle grazing their way slowly across the valley. They began to ride that way.

'Up there,' Holly said, waving with her right hand, 'is Dos Picos. We've a tangle of brush-clotted canyons and cacti and brambles up in there, and a lot of lost beef.'

'I've heard about it,' Trinity said, and Holly gave him a look of close scrutiny.

'How? When?'

'Just last night. Some of the hands were talking.'

At Holly's look he smiled and said, 'I told you that I've been asked to look around and keep my ears open.'

'By whom — Russell?'

'He's a little overwhelmed right now,' Trinity said, without really answering her question.

'Yes,' Holly said, 'so are we all.' Then she heeled her little pony into a brisk lope and they approached the cattle herd at a quicker pace. The animals had not yet been sorted into a trail herd. One and two-year olds, too young for such a drive, mingled with the herd and Trinity even saw a few bulls, too valuable to be sold for beef, among them. He mentioned this to Holly.

'I know. We're just finishing up looking for strays up along Dos Picas. When they're all gathered, the men will start dividing the herd.'

'That's a tough job,' Trinity said from experience. The bulls would not like anyone interfering in their domain; none of the cattle would be eager to move off what they now considered to be their home range.

They walked their horses among the cattle. They all seemed to be sleek and fat, bright-eyed, well-fed and watered. Even the two-dozen or so longhorns among them. From time to time Trinity leaned out of the saddle to stroke an animal's coat. There were no lesions, no scabbed sores. These animals had been well tended. The army, it seemed, had made a good bargain when it chose to purchase its beef from Owl.

'How many are you taking?' Trinity asked as they left the herd.

'One hundred and fifty,' Holly said. 'The army has already built holding pens near Fort Bridger. It's my understanding that a lot of them will be used to barter with the Indians, though I don't know much about that. It doesn't concern Owl. The army sent a young officer around to inspect the herd a month or so ago, and he was quite pleased with them.'

Trinity nodded. He had gathered as much from his conversation with Tonio in the stable.

'What was his name?'

'I'm not sure. Father dealt with him. I think it was Lieutenant Ross — something like that.' They had halted their horses again on a low grassy knoll from which they could look down on the red and white backs of the grazing cattle. To the east, a mile or so away, Trinity could see a small group of Owl riders approaching them.

'Is there anyone among you who doesn't want the cattle sold?' Trinity asked. Holly had removed her hat again, and swirls of red hair crossed her eyes as they flashed uncertainly.

'What do you mean? Who wouldn't want to sell them?'

'I just wondered,' Trinity said weakly. Holly replanted her hat, more firmly.

'That's what they were raised for. They are the money on the hoof that the Owl needs to continue. *I* want to sell them, I'll tell you that. Our savings have gotten pretty low. Millicent doesn't give a hang about anything that goes on around here so long as the money to pamper herself continues to flow in. She, of course, wants to sell them. She always needs money, more money . . . she wants these to go through. Not that there's a choice: we have already contracted with the government and they're not fond of people who back out of sales contracts. Your question makes no sense. Of course we want to deliver the herd, as soon as possible.'

She started her pony down the knoll, and Trinity followed, his eyes flickering toward the approaching cowboys — probably the bunch being sent up into the tangle of canyons surrounding Dos Picos to look for strays.

Trinity and Holly rode in silence for a way. He found himself admiring the way she sat on her saddle, the erect line of her back beneath that red-checked cotton shirt she wore.

'What about Earl?' he persisted. Holly frowned at him.

'What do you mean? Are you still talking about who might not wish to sell the herd?'

'Yes, I am. They say that Earl has his own spread down in Texas. Maybe he could use more cattle.'

'From what I know of it, my brother's ranch is water-poor. He's already running all the cattle his land can support, and doing well at it,' Holly answered, snapping at him — her voice had grown sharper.

'And Vincent Battles?' he ventured.

Holly's eyes hardened. They were gold, now that he was paying more intention — oddly gold eyes, now sharp with displeasure.

'You don't know Vincent Battles.'

'No, I don't. Tell me about him.'

She shook her head fractionally. Was she in love with Battles? Trinity knew that at one time Battles had worked for Owl. Until when? Was it possible that the old man, Lewis Bates, had sent him away for some indiscretion or other?

'I'll tell you what you need to know for your line of enquiry,' Holly finally answered as they entered a small stand of scattered pine trees. 'Though I don't know why you are so curious. Who are you, anyway?'

It was Trinity's turn not to answer. After a few minutes, as their horses plodded on silently — their hoofbeats muffled by fallen pine needles and the cool breeze drifting through the dark pines — Holly continued.

'Vincent Battles is only interested in making some money for himself and his men. Do you think he has it in mind to steal an entire herd of cattle and drive them five hundred miles to Mexico unseen, untracked? If no one else followed him, the army would be after him within a day or two — you can't run fast or far with a herd that size which isn't even broken to the trail yet.'

'No,' Trinity admitted, 'I guess you can't.'

'Besides, Vince is a good friend of the family. A very good friend of mine,' she said with more emphasis. That silenced Trinity.

They rode on without speaking, Trinity mulling over all that he had heard, Holly apparently still considering Trinity. She had not failed to notice that her question. 'Who are you?' had gone unanswered. Trinity was acting oddly, asking a lot of probing questions for some drifting man Russ had happened to meet along the trail and hired on out of gratitude.

They emerged from the cool of the pine forest on to a sun-bright slope.

There was a little-used trail which Holly must have known of, making its uncertain way past a stand of craggy yellow boulders toward the flats beyond. The Owl Ranch house was visible, a mile or so away. Holly drew her paint pony up briefly in the shadows cast by the huge boulders.

'All right,' she said with determination. 'You ask more questions than you have answered, mister. I would like to know — '

At that moment the face of the rock behind them exploded with splinter and dust. The echo of a rifle followed immediately. Trinity reached toward Holly, snatched her from the saddle with one arm and rolled to the ground with her, as the horses shied away and the day filled with gunfire.

4

Trinity kept his hand on the back of Holly's head, holding her down as bullets continued to spatter against the face of the rocks and ricochet off wildly, spraying them with rock fragments and dust. Peering into the harsh sunlight, Trinity could see nothing of their attacker. It would have done him little good, anyway. He held only his handgun. The piebald had danced away from the ruckus with his Winchester in its saddle scabbard.

'Why don't you shoot back?' Holly demanded.

'It would be like throwing stones at this distance, with a Colt,' he answered. The shooting continued for another minute or so, the length of time it would have taken the man, whoever he was, to empty the magazine of his rifle.

Trinity continued to squint toward

the low, bleak knoll he thought the shots were coming from, but he saw nothing, not even a trail of gunsmoke which the breeze would dissipate as soon as it rose.

But far across the valley he saw the bunch of Owl riders he had assumed were riding to the Dos Picos to hunt for strays. They had heard the shots, apparently, and had quickened their ponies' pace. After a minute, apparently frightened off by the cowboys, the rifleman halted his assault. Trinity sat up, his pistol still in his hand. Holly was beside him, hatless, her hair spiked with burrs. She leaned her head against his shoulder and sat waiting beside him.

There were no more shots from their ambusher. The cowhands had slowed and veered off toward their original destination with the cessation of fire.

'So, that is that,' Holly said, turning frightened golden eyes up toward Trinity.

'It seems so. Give it another few minutes, then we'll collect our horses.'

The cool morning had grown warm with the ascension of the sun, and insects now hummed around them. The cowboys had vanished into the distance, riding toward Dos Picos.

'Trinity?' Holly said.

'Yes?' He brushed a strand of hair from her forehead. She didn't object to the gesture.

'Who was it, do you think? Who did they want to kill — you or me?'

It was a good question. Trinity had assumed that he was the target — but who and why eluded him. Surely Willie Meese had not carried a bunkhouse fight to this extreme, not while his boss lady was riding with Trinity.

'You think it was you who was the target — don't you, Holly?'

'Yes, but I don't know who.'

He fixed his eyes on hers. His grip involuntarily tightened on her arm as he held her to him. She did not pull away. 'Who would want to kill you, Holly? Why?'

'Money,' she answered simply. 'I am

about to become an heiress, Trinity, in case you haven't realized it. The Owl is worth quite a bit.'

'Yes, but — '

She went on, speaking past his interruption.

'None of us has seen the will Father made yet. A lawyer named McAfee is coming up here from Sage to read it.'

'I was told that in your family the eldest son always inherited.'

'My father was not that hidebound in his thinking,' Holly insisted.

'You think someone suspects that the Owl might fall to you?'

'Or a large portion of it,' she said. Trinity had risen to his feet. He dusted his pants off and offered a hand to Holly, drawing her erect. They both stood looking eastward at the knoll where the shots were believed to have originated.

'But certainly Russell wouldn't . . . ' Trinity said in defense of his new-found friend.

'Oh, I don't know!' Holly said in

exasperation obviously fed by fear. 'He deserted from the army and managed to get here the day Father died. How do any of us know that Father really sent for him?'

'I can't believe that.'

'Oh, Russ has always been a great liar. When we were younger . . . and then there's Earl, of course. Did I tell you he arrived late last night? Well, he did. Saying quite a bit about troubles he was having down on his Texas spread — lack of water being chief among them, plus sporadic Indian raids and a squabble with some Mexican land-owners.'

Trinity frowned. It sounded as if Earl needed money and needed it quickly.

'And don't forget Millicent,' Holly went on. 'I know she likes to present herself as a kitten curled up before the fire, but she can shoot, believe me.'

'Whoever it was,' Trinity said, 'we're both lucky he wasn't that good of a shot.'

They walked downslope to gather up

the reins to their frightened horses. Trinity was still thinking of the possible identity of the man behind the sights. He did not believe it could be Millicent; that would not be her way of doing things. If she were disposed to harm Holly, she would find a more subtle method than clambering up through the rocks and emptying a Winchester magazine at her sister. What about Vincent Battles whom Holly still apparently held in high esteem? Trinity didn't trust the man, didn't like his looks, however irrational that feeling might be. Plus there was still Willie Meese — maybe the man was crazy enough to try to take his revenge on Trinity with a long gun, Holly's proximity be damned.

'It's quite a tangle,' Trinity said as he swung aboard the now-calmed piebald. He watched Holly pull herself into the paint pony's saddle.

'I know you wondered about the snappish mood I was in yesterday when I met you,' Holly said as they rode easily toward home. 'But my father had just died. I loved him, of course, but I had also always counted on his savvy to run the ranch, every facet of it. Earl was gone, Millicent was no help. I was left alone to try to manage the Owl — a job which, I must admit, overwhelmed me. The day to day decisions left me a babbling fool. How I was to handle the sale of the herd and lead a trail drive was more than daunting. I just couldn't handle it. I knew it, and sent for Vincent Battles. He had worked for us before, and I knew he was a man of experience. I decided to leave it all in his lap for the time being. What else was there to do? I was like a passenger on a train thrust into the role of engineer — I had an idea what had to be done, but no real comprehension of the nature of the beast.'

'You did what you could. I don't blame you for being confused and angry.'

'Then out of the blue, Russ shows up! If Father sent for him, I didn't know anything about it. And he dragged you along with him, Trinity.' Again those golden eyes met his. 'And I don't know a thing about you. I know you're not telling me the whole truth about who you are.'

'Just a friend,' Trinity said as they neared the house.

'Just a friend of Russell's.'

'Just a friend,' he repeated to the girl with the golden eyes, as they rode past the lone blue spruce tree to the front of the white house, where sorrow and confusion still reigned.

Russell Bates stood on the front porch, watching their return, his eyes narrowed with puzzlement. He was dressed now in fresh clothes — a white shirt and black jeans and he was shaven, his hair slicked down with water or oil or both.

'You two have made friends, have you?' Russell asked as he caught Holly's paint horse by the bridle so she could swing down more easily.

'We met on the trail,' was all Holly

said, leaving her brother to match her own explanation with that he had given to her about meeting Trinity. 'Where's Earl?'

'Storming around somewhere. He more or less told me and Vincent Battles both to stay out of matters, that he would handle Owl affairs, he being the more experienced cattleman as well as Lew Bates's oldest son.'

'What did Vincent have to say about that?' Holly asked.

'Well, I don't use that kind of language, but he told Earl in no uncertain terms that you had hired him on as foreman, and he was going to do the job until you told him he was fired. They went at it tooth and nail for a long time before Vincent just threw up his hands and went out the back door, slamming it shut behind him.'

'I don't like that,' Holly said.

'It was pretty predictable,' Trinity put in.

'If I'd known Father was going to pass away so soon — '

'You wouldn't have invited Vince Battles up here?' Russell asked.

'Wouldn't I have? I don't know.' She shook her head. 'But if Millicent hadn't invited Earl, we wouldn't have this — two lobo wolves, each trying to assume the boss dog position.'

'Millicent couldn't have *not* told Earl,' Russell said. 'You would have done the same thing — how could Earl be kept away from Father's deathbed? There are family obligations.'

'It's all about the will,' Holly said in as sharp a tone as any she had used the day before, 'Earl doesn't care about the trail drive or Owl — unless it is bequeathed to him.'

'That's not fair, Holly,' Russell said.

'Isn't it?' she spat back. 'Then where was Earl all those years when Father was weakening each day, trying to make sure that the ranch was kept up, his legacy a rich one?'

'I don't know. Earl wanted to do something on his own, I expect. I know I did. Both of us had arguments with

69

Father over our decisions, but a son can't be held a slave to his father's dreams.'

'You preferred to be a soldier?' Holly said with mockery.

'I liked the idea. It represented freedom.'

'A lot of freedom you'll have when they catch you and throw you in the stockade,' Holly said hotly. But she was running out of steam now, her voice not so fiery. Trinity thought that she was considering that matters on the Owl had gotten much worse, not better, now that her brothers and Vincent Battles had appeared.

'Why are you here anyway?' Holly asked Russell. 'You can see we have enough men around to manage the drive.'

'I'm here,' Russell told her stiffly, 'because my father sent for me. I don't know if it was the drive or something else that he wished me to take care of.'

'What else?' Holly waved her hands overhead. 'What could there be?'

'I don't know,' Russell answered in the same wooden tone. 'But I mean to find out and see that my father's last wishes are addressed.'

'You're crazy, Russ, you know that? Unless this is all something you've fabricated to duck out from under army tedium.'

'I have not fabricated my father's death,' Russell said coldly. Now, he too, had grown tired of this pointless argument, Trinity thought. He stood by, his horse's reins in his hand, studying the two — brother and sister — so alike despite their differing points of view.

Russell Bates was not quite finished. 'As for having enough men to make me superfluous on the Owl — you have enough men. You have more than enough. You have, as you said, two snarling wolves fighting over the pack. You also should know that Earl brought half a dozen Texas roughnecks with him. I would hate to see how they will get along with Vincent Battles's crew when they find out they have been

71

hired on to do the same job.'

'That sounds a little ominous,' Holly said. 'I'll tell Vincent and Earl to do something about it, though I don't see what can be done.'

'Nor do I,' Russell said. 'They both want control of things, and each has his own contingent of men.'

'It could lead to fighting,' Holly said thoughtfully, nibbling on her lower lip.

'It could lead to a lot more than that. It could lead to shooting, and you know it.'

'I don't suppose there's any way to separate the two factions,' Trinity said. Both looked at him, shaking their heads.

'There's only the one bunkhouse. Father always meant to build another; he always expected the ranch to grow and prosper. But it was another of those projects we never got around to,' Russell said.

'The men will be fighting just for a place to sleep,' Trinity commented.

'I'll talk to my brother and Vincent,'

Holly promised. 'Maybe something can be worked out,' she said knowing that it could not. She now lifted her eyes to Trinity. Gold eyes. 'You must move into the big house, Trinity. I know there will be more trouble for you if you stay in the bunkhouse now.'

Russell let his eyes flicker from his sister to Trinity. There was a question in them. Only yesterday his sister had been insistent that Trinity stay away from the house and bunk with the cowhands. What had changed her mind?

'Your brother may not like that,' Trinity said gravely, 'or Vincent Battles.'

'I don't care what they like! It's my house,' Holly announced to the world, turning to look at the face of the two-storey white house, 'and I'll invite whatever guests I like into it.'

Then she turned and walked up on to the porch and into the house, her back rigid. Russell smiled at Trinity. 'It looks like you made a conquest.'

'Not in any ordinary sense,' Trinity

said. 'Are you going to hold that horse forever, or help me stable them up? I'm through riding for the day.'

As they turned away from it, they could hear raised voices in the house. 'Just be careful, Trinity,' Russell told him. 'I don't know what you have in mind, but Holly is a volatile little keg of gunpowder. Besides, Vincent Battles has already staked his claim to her, in his own mind at least. You'd be dealing with a sort of hell if you tried to see that matters are arranged differently.'

'Who says I have anything like that in mind?' Trinity said gruffly as they reached the stable. 'You've got too much imagination, Russell.'

As they groomed and put away their horses, Trinity related what had happened that morning to him and Holly out on the range. Roger, the stableman, dozed in the corner, perched on a wooden barrel.

'I don't like the sound of that,' Russell said, brushing the back of Holly's paint pony. Over it's back, he studied Trinity, busy with his piebald. 'Who do you think it was?'

'I really don't know. You don't suppose it could have been Willie Meese, trying to even the score?'

'See that buckskin in the first stall?' Russell asked. 'That's Meese's horse. It hasn't been ridden today. Cooky told me that Willie was having trouble just breathing, his nose being broken again.'

'All right — that eliminates him,' Trinity said, placing his currycomb aside. 'Trouble is, that leaves us with a lot of suspects, doesn't it? And no known motive.'

'And you don't know who he was shooting at.' Russell's head bowed in thought. 'It had to be you, didn't it, Trinity? I mean what man in his right mind goes around trying to kill a woman in this part of the country? He'd never live to hang for it — he'd be torn to bits.'

'It had to be me,' Trinity said unconvinced.

'Unless someone stood to gain from

killing Holly, is that what you're thinking?'

'I didn't say that,' Trinity answered.

'You didn't say it because if that were so, it would have to be one of the family — or Vincent Battles. Or . . . me,' Russell said, his eyes pleading for his friend's trust.

'It wasn't you, Russell,' Trinity said, walking nearer to let his hand drop on Russell Bates's shoulder. 'I know that.'

'Thanks, Trinity,' Russell said with feeling. Then his face flushed slightly and his eyes brightened. 'You've got to help me figure out who was shooting at my sister, and why. Whoever it was might be tempted to try again.'

'I agree,' Trinity said, 'but you're laying a lot on me, Russell. You've given me two different and difficult jobs: to find out what your father needed done that was so important he asked you to desert your army post to do it, and to discover who might be trying to kill your sister — if she was the target. That is a lot to ask.'

76

'I know it is.' Russell removed his hat and ran his fingers through his now uncombed hair. He was agitated and had the right to be. Had it occurred to him that he also might be a target of the killer? Trinity assumed he had, but his concern was obviously only for Holly. 'But don't you think — ?'

'That the two matters — the concerns of your father and the shooting — might have the same cause? Yes, I do. What I don't have,' Trinity told him, 'is a handle on why it is happening. Do you think someone has already viewed your father's will and found it unfavorable toward him?'

'I don't see how. The lawyer, McAfee, has his offices down in Sage.'

'There could have been another copy,' Trinity reminded him. 'You've been away from home quite awhile. If there was such a document only your sisters would be likely to know. You'd better ask them.'

The two men walked out into the sunlight, brilliant after the shadows of the barn.

'You know where this all points, don't you?' Russell said, his eyes fixed on the tall, blue spruce tree in the yard of the Bates's house where a dozen or so raucous crows had decided to congregate. 'Directly at one of the other family members. Me, Earl or — '

'Holly told me that Millicent was well acquainted with firearms.'

'Yes, well so are a lot of people and they don't all go around shooting their sisters.' He shook his head. 'I can't believe it could have been Millicent.'

'Has she taken a horse out this morning? You could ask Tonio.'

'I won't!' Russell said defiantly. 'I won't insult Millicent like that. I tell you she's not that sort of woman.'

'A lot of people who aren't 'that sort' have found themselves driven to it in extraordinary circumstances,' Trinity reminded him.

Russell sighed, shrugged. 'That's so,' he conceded. 'All of this seems to point to Earl, doesn't it? After all, he was expecting to inherit all of Owl one day.'

78

'He still may be,' Trinity speculated. 'Since no one admits to seeing the will your father wrote. But,' he reminded Russell, 'Earl certainly wasn't around when Dalton Remy was hanged, was he?'

'No. Earl has only just arrived. But, Trinity, Earl was with me or around me all morning in the house. He can't possibly have been the one who shot at you and Holly.'

'You're right,' Trinity agreed. 'But I've heard he brought in at least six men with him. One of them could have been dispatched to do the job.'

'You won't accept the fact that it could have been an outsider,' Russell said dismally. He was trying to convince himself that it could be someone outside the family who had attempted to kill Holly Bates — if she had been the target Trinity believed she was. Who besides Willie Meese had a grudge against Trinity?

'We'd better get to the bottom of this before someone is killed,' Russell said.

'I mean to — if there's time,' Trinity said. 'Who's this?' he asked as both men stood looking at a surrey, drawn by a high-stepping red roan and sending up dust as it made its way towards the Bates house.

'Someone who might have an answer to a part of this,' Russell said with an expression that was part pained smile, part grimace. 'If I'm not mistaken, that is the lawyer, Hugh McAfee from Sage, coming to read Father's will.'

'Aren't you going in?' Trinity asked as Russell remained fixed where he stood.

'We have a chore to do first — if you'll help me. My father's grave has yet to be dug.' Russell frowned deeply. 'I want to get him beneath the ground so that he can't see any of what is about to happen.'

5

An hour later, both men dirty and sweaty were washing up in the kitchen as a frowning Alicia watched them. Tonio had helped them maneuver the body of Lew Bates down the stairs from his bedroom and out of the house to be put down in the cold earth beneath the cottonwoods behind the house. No one else had appeared to ask them a question — maybe no one wanted to admit what was happening.

The inner door to the kitchen slammed open as Trinity stood rolling his sleeves down. Russell was still drying his hands.

'What took you so long?' Vincent Battles demanded from the doorway. 'I've buried six men in half the time you took.'

Russell Bates was thinking that it was probably true. The cold-eyed cattle man waited impatiently for them to finish up as Alicia tried to protect the food she was preparing for dinner from contamination.

'That lawyer has been standing around in the front room for hours. You, at least, Russell, should want to hear what he has to tell us.' Trinity wondered at Vincent Battles's own eagerness. The wolfish man seemed to feel that there was something in it for him. Was that perhaps the reason he had been catering to Holly? Wanting to have a part of her share, whatever that might prove to be.

Following Battles out, they crossed the front room to what Trinity guessed had been Lew Bates's office when he was alive. Around the room, the others waited. The lawyer, Hugh McAfee, tall and narrow and wearing spectacles, stood behind a massive carved oaken desk. Holly and Millicent occupied the two thickly padded black leather chairs facing him. Standing against the wall near a glass-fronted book case stood a broad-shouldered, pale-haired man. This had to be Earl Bates. He resembled none of the others. Square head, hair trimmed to within a half inch of his scalp, thick in the chest, he resembled nothing more than a Dutch teamster. He had sharp blue eyes which flickered to Trinity, revealing displeasure.

'Who are you? This meeting is for family only. That means you may leave, Battles.' His eyes returned to Trinity. 'I asked who you are.'

'This is my friend, Trinity,' Russell said.

'Family only,' Earl Bates said again.

'Whose rule is that?' Russell wanted to know. 'You're not running these proceedings, Earl.' Earl Bates frowned and said, 'I see that time in the army has given you a little backbone, Russ, but I want him out of here.' He pointed toward the door where Vincent Battles had exited.

The man behind the desk spoke for the first time. 'If it will save any time,' Hugh McAfee suggested, 'why don't the four of you just put it to a vote. I

83

myself have no objections to this man remaining.'

'I want Trinity here as well,' Holly said. Earl's eyebrows drew together in surprise.

'All right,' he said grudgingly. 'You know how I feel about it. What do you say, Millicent?'

'I'm sure it doesn't matter to me one way or the other,' Millicent replied, lifting one shoulder in a ladylike shrug which was barely visible beneath the fabric of the black dress she wore on this day.

'Then stay — and keep quiet,' Earl said. This was a man obviously used to having his own way in everything. 'Let's get this over with, McAfee.'

Hugh McAfee seated himself behind the broad desk and drew a sheaf of papers from his black leather portmanteau. 'If I may begin . . . '

He droned on for quite awhile, using 'whereas' and 'in respect to' frequently as the others fidgeted. McAfee had a way of speaking without seeming to move his lips. The lawyer's words hissed out between his teeth, making understanding him even more difficult. Trinity had not really been listening, but he could see by the flush on his face that Earl Bates was growing angry. Holly only nodded her understanding. Millicent seemed to be in another world. Russell craned his neck forward as if trying to comprehend the legal text being read to them.

'Do you want to boil all of that down for us, McAfee?' Earl Bates asked when the lawyer had finished.

'Weren't you listening?' McAfee seemed to feel put upon.

'I was listening; I just didn't like what I thought I heard,' Earl said in a gravelly tone.

'Simply,' Hugh McAfee told them, looking from one face to the other. 'You all have an equal share in the Owl Ranch. As far as cash reserves — there seem to be few.'

'Until the cattle are delivered to Fort Bridger,' Holly said.

'Well, by God!' Earl exploded. 'I rode all this way for nothing? I need cash to keep my own ranch going, to pay my men. Look, McAfee, can I sell my share of the property?'

'No,' McAfee said, snapping his leather case shut. He pushed his spectacles up on his nose with his thumb. 'Everyone would have to agree to such a sale. No one has a specific section of land apportioned to him. It's a common asset. You own one quarter of the ranch and future profits.'

'Future profits don't do me much good right now — I've got cattle dying off because of loss of water, men quitting because I can't make their pay.'

Apparently, Trinity was thinking, Earl Bates had overextended himself buying too much land and bringing in so many cattle that the land could not support them. It was not an uncommon occurrence down on the west Texas lands where rain was always unpredictable.

Earl swallowed hard as if he had a

mouthful of ball bearings and walked from the room, his troubles weighing heavily on him. As he passed through the door, Trinity caught sight of Vincent Battles, leaning against the fireplace waiting hopefully.

The reading of the will, then, had affected none of their lives. Holly and Millicent would continue to live on the Owl; Earl Bates, disappointed, would probably return to his Texas spread to wait for his share of the profits from the trail herd. Russell was still in trouble as deep as before without an idea what his father had wanted from him.

Trinity turned and started out toward the back door. He could hear Earl Bates and Vincent Battles going at it.

'I'm using my men on that drive,' Earl was saying in a bullying voice. 'They need their pay, and I mean to be at Fort Bridger when that herd is delivered. I mean to make sure I collect my share of the sale.'

'Holly has already hired me and my

crew to do that job, Bates,' Battles answered with firmness. 'Why don't you just hit leather and line out for the Texas country. No one needs you around here.'

It seemed that the argument was likely to continue for a long while. Trinity continued toward the kitchen door. Vincent Battles caught his movement from the corner of his eye and called out to him.

'You! Trinity! You can't go on just lazing around here. Tomorrow you put on your spurs and get to work like the rest of us.'

This was one order Earl Bates didn't feel like objecting to. He stood silently by, his eyes no less fierce than those of Battles.

'I'll be ready,' Trinity said. After all, it was only fair that he earn his bread. Of course the idea could be to get him out on the range alone, but he couldn't simply dismiss the Owl Ranch's foreman, shaky as Vincent Battles's own position might be. Holly had emerged from the conference room and she stopped Trinity. Taking his arm, she said just loudly enough for Bates and Vincent Battles to hear: 'Don't forget, Trinity, you're staying in the house from now on.'

Trinity nodded and kept going. He needed not so much as to be by himself as to be away from the arguments and endless bickering going on within the house. Holly would try to talk to the two men who both insisted they be in charge, but it was unlikely she would get anywhere with them. Trinity had to admit that each had a point — Battles had been sent for to manage the drive and hired on as ranch foreman. Earl was part-owner of the ranch. Leave it up to them! Trinity opened the kitchen door and walked out to where a cool wind was blowing.

He walked a little way out into the cottonwood grove. The barren branches criss-crossed the earth with shadows. Damp spongy leaves were underfoot. He paused for a minute at Lew Bates's freshly-dug grave, pondering his own mortality, then walked toward the barn where his horse was stabled. He did not want to go riding, but the horses on this day would make more pleasant company than the humans.

He was careful to give the bunkhouse a wide berth, but it did him no good. As he reached the barn, Willie Meese, leading his buckskin horse and another man were coming out. Trinity nodded, but said nothing. Meese tried to screw his face up into a vengeful mask, but the sticking plaster he wore across the bridge of his nose ruined whatever effect he was trying for.

'I know that man,' Trinity heard Meese's companion say as he entered the barn. When Trinity glanced back, he saw the new man watching him with a fixed gaze.

'From where?' Meese asked the man whose name was Plimford and had just arrived from Texas with Earl Bates's crew.

'I'm not sure,' Plimford said, scratching at his narrow chin. 'But I seen him before somewhere — he's bad news, I think, Willie.'

The two then moved away from the barn, speaking in low voices. Trinity cursed under his breath. He knew Dave Plimford as well. The beanstalk of a man had been involved in some shady dealings down near Ruidoso. It wouldn't have mattered, but Trinity did not wish to be discovered just yet. He had hardly begun with his work.

Roger, the stableman was not there. From what Tonio had said of him, and from what Trinity himself had observed, it was likely that Roger was sleeping off his whisky load somewhere. Tonio, Trinity saw as his eyes adjusted to the semi-darkness, was in one of the back stalls, tending to a leggy blue roan.

'Hello, Tonio,' Trinity said, walking that way past the curious eyes of the horses.

'Oh, it's you. Are you riding out?'

'Not again today, I don't think.' He watched the boy run a grooming brush over the blue roan. The animal's hide

91

quivered under the brush. Obviously the horse was enjoying the attention. 'Whose horse is that?' Trinity asked.

'This one belongs to Earl Bates,' the kid said. 'I am taking special care of him in case Mr Bates inherits the Owl and he might make me permanent stable boy.'

Trinity did not tell the boy that Earl Bates would not be inheriting the ranch, not now. 'Your mother doesn't need you today?'

'Not now — she will call me if she does. Usually she don't need me again until just before supper.'

'Those two men who just left . . . ?' Trinity began. Tonio laughed.

'Willie and the new man? Willie was telling the new man how you jumped him and broke his nose.'

'Was he?' Trinity said. 'I just noticed that they took their horses out and it seems kind of late in the day to start work. I wondered if you might have an idea where they were headed.'

Tonio lowered his brush. 'Sure,' he

answered. 'I know where they're going. They were talking about it as if I wasn't here. They're going out to look at the other herd.'

The other herd? Trinity wasn't really that surprised. He had expected that he might find something like that, but it seemed such a bold risk. He asked Tonio:

'Do you have any idea where this other herd might be?'

'Naw, they didn't say nothing about that, and I don't spend much time on the range. I'm happier around here, Trinity.'

'I know.' Trinity watched thoughtfully for a while longer as Tonio finished his grooming of the blue roan. 'Tell me, Tonio, where is the smith's shack?'

'You need something fixed? No one is over there now. Our old smith left to live in town, over in Sage. He said he was too old for the job. That was last year sometime.'

'I just wanted to look around,' Trinity told the boy.

'What you do is go behind the bunkhouse toward the pigpen. There's two buildings out that way. The first is the smoke house. A few hundred feet farther along, you'll find the smith's shack.'

Thanking Tonio, Trinity set off in the direction indicated. Finding the pigpen took no effort at all. The hogs could be smelled fifty yards away. The wind was growing more chilly. One pig, fresh from the wallow followed Trinity along through the fence, grunting and twitching its nose. Trinity smiled — maybe he smelled as bad to the pigs as they did to him.

The smoke house was low, squat, and windowless of course. Beside it, running from corner to corner was a planting box which held green onions, garlic and a small shrub with tiny blue flowers which a grass widow woman over in Abilene had once explained to Trinity was rosemary. With sage as abundant as grass, there were enough herbs here to season about anything.

Trinity paused to take a peek inside the smoke-house. From the dark ceiling he could see two dozen hams hanging, and coils of sausage draped along the walls — the purpose behind the herbs he had seen outside — along with sides of bacon and paddle wide strips of beef jerky. It all reminded Trinity that he was very hungry — he had had only those biscuits for breakfast and he had given Holly one of them.

Holly had invited him to sleep in the house, but said nothing about supper. Maybe with Tonio's influence, Trinity could convince Alicia to make him a sandwich.

His head came around at the sound of approaching horses.

Some of the Owl riders were returning to the bunkhouse after working all day on the range. They would find Earl Bates's Texas riders inside, perhaps on their bunks. This was a recipe for disaster and Trinity knew he wanted no part of it. The two factions would surely clash.

He continued along the path and eventually found the small smith's shack set by the side of the road. It hadn't been used for some time but still Trinity's nostrils caught the scent of slag and iron shavings. He approached the shack and opened the door, finding that it swung easily open on oiled hinges. He frowned slightly at that. According to Tonio, the blacksmith had been gone for some time. Well, he considered, perhaps others used it on occasion.

Entering, he saw the cold forge, an anvil and some heavy short-handled sledges hanging from pins on the wall. Trinity began poking through the tool barrels there, some of the tools — a split shovel, a broken pickaxe — waiting for repairs that would never come. A row of iron tyres for the wagon wheels leaned against another wall.

Near the anvil, Trinity found discarded two-inch long arcs of iron. He crouched and examined them, frowning. They exactly resembled the loops of metal the smith had fashioned to represent the eyes of the Owl brand, which was what they were.

Also on the ground was an intact Owl branding iron which seemed to have been damaged when someone tried to hammer these pieces free. A one-eyed owl watched as Trinity's frown deepened. Trinity played with the arcs of metal, placing them together in various ways until a bit of nearly-forgotten knowledge rose to illuminate him.

He knew what they were doing with the other herd.

Rising, he dusted off his knees and slipped out of the smith's shack, into the cool of settling dusk. A shout from near the bunkhouse drew his gaze that way. Two men he did not know were going at it with fists and boots. The group of men, gathered to watch, were bunched together in two distinct clusters — Earl's Texas roughnecks and Vincent Battles's cowhands. It was too predictable.

He wondered if Holly had had any luck in negotiating a peace between the two cattlemen. It seemed unlikely — both were obstinate, proud and angry. Trinity started to walk that way. Holly, Russell, or Trinity himself had to do something, and do it soon.

The Owl was teetering on the brink of total collapse.

6

Holly was in the kitchen, seated at the table, watching as Alicia worked over the steaming stove. Holly's golden eyes flashed at him.

'Where have you been?' she demanded in a tone Trinity didn't care for.

'Staying out of the way,' he said, taking a chair out to sit facing her. Alicia cast him a sidelong glance with her suspicious black eyes. 'There's nothing I can add to the discussion.'

'Discussion!' Holly barked. 'Is that what you call this warfare between Vincent and Earl?'

'I take it they haven't come to any agreement,' Trinity answered calmly, and Holly's temper subsided slightly.

'They don't want to,' Holly said miserably. 'They just want to puff up and pose and make as much noise as possible.'

'I know you can't fire Vincent Battles,' Trinity said.

'Not after I practically begged him for his help and he collected those men and rode all the way up here!' Holly said.

'And no one is going to convince Earl to ride back to Texas — not until he gets his share of the profit from the cattle sale.'

'No, and he has as much right to his share as Russell, Millicent and I do,' Holly said miserably. This was all getting too much for her, Trinity knew. He stretched out his hand and touched the back of hers gently.

'This won't last for ever,' he told her.

'I know,' she said, turning her eyes down. Her voice was much softer now — the girl needed a lot of soothing attention. 'To me it's all about saving the Owl, and I need to sell those cattle to do that. To them,' she waved a disparaging hand, 'it all seems to be about the profit to be made.'

'Of course it is,' Trinity agreed, 'but

100

you'd better tell them to take off their sparring gloves right now, and at least make a temporary truce of some kind — because if they don't step in and calm down their crews, they'll have to make a trail drive with men that have broken arms and legs and battered skulls.'

'Has it gotten that bad?' Holly asked with deep distress.

'Not yet, but it's already started.' He told her briefly about the fight he had seen outside the bunkhouse. 'Once any man pulls a gun, it's all over.'

'Surely it won't come to that,' Holly said.

'Holly, you know as well as I do that these are rough men and any one of them could be goaded into it if he thinks he's getting a raw deal.'

She rose immediately. 'I'll speak to them again — if I can get them to quiet down enough so that they'll listen to me.' She started towards the door, paused and said over her shoulder. 'Supper's in an hour or so. You have time to wash up.'

Again Alicia shot a glance at Trinity; again she said nothing. He guessed the cook liked to know how many portions to cook before the table was to be set.

Trinity had gotten to his feet when Millicent Bates, looking cool and other-worldly, swept into the steamy room. There was a cup in her hand. She glanced at Trinity, half-smiled, and said to the cook: 'I seem to have run out of tea again, Alicia. Will you brew me some?' Trinity was glad he could not read the cook's lips as Millicent glided away again. He did hear Alicia mutter: 'Never enough tea. What does she do with all the tea? Water the plants?'

He took that as a cue to leave. He turned and headed toward the back door just as Tonio arrived to help out with serving the supper. The two merely nodded to each other, and Trinity, tugging his collar up against the chill of evening, walked to the pump to wash his face and hands. Far to the north thunder grumbled and a few low-lying stars were hidden behind the screen of approaching clouds. That was all they needed — a storm to lift everyone's spirits.

* * *

There wasn't much said at the dining room table on that evening. Tonio bustled in and out, taking away used dishes, serving new portions. The kid was dressed in neat black trousers and a crisp white shirt. He smiled frequently, but Trinity could tell that he wished he were back in the stable among his horse friends.

The table, covered with a white linen cloth, held Vincent Battles, seated at one end, Earl Bates at the other. Both glowering, their attention apparently only on their food on this evening. Russell, seated in the chair opposite Trinity's, remarked that it smelled like rain to him and it would be a hell of a way to have to start a herd that was not trail broken on its way west.

Nobody responded. Holly, seated next to Russell and delicately picking at her food, asked her brother, 'You are still planning on going with us to Fort Bridger, Russ?'

'It's necessary,' he answered. 'After the herd is safely delivered . . . I'll just have to let the army do whatever they have planned for me.'

'I don't like cabbage,' Millicent said. Her plate was covered with a buttered wedge of cabbage, boiled potatoes and sliced rare beef in gravy. She might have finished three or four bites of meat since sitting down.

'It suits me,' Holly said. 'I'm hungry.'

'You should be. Why didn't you show up for breakfast this morning?' Russell asked.

'I just felt like an early ride.'

Trinity glanced at her. That wasn't what she had told him. Holly had said that she didn't care for Alicia's Spanish-style eggs. Then why had she been out on the range — following him? That seemed unlikely, but it was possible.

'Where's that boy?' Earl thundered, leaning back to hold his belly with both hands. His plate was empty. 'I want some more beef and potatoes.' His eyes shifted to Holly, 'Still plan on going along on the drive, Sis?'

'I pretty much have to,' was her answer. 'Father and I were the co-signers of the contract with the army. And,' she said with her eyes down on her plate, 'I want to make sure that the Owl is paid in full.'

'I still need my pay,' Vincent Battles said, his fork halfway to his mouth.

'Of course,' Holly said pleasantly. 'As soon as we return from Bridger. That will be time enough to settle financial matters.'

'You, Battles,' Earl Bates said, glaring at him down the long table, 'You don't have to go any further with this. I don't need you on the drive; I've got enough men. Why don't you hang around the Owl and take care of things here? We don't need two trail bosses.'

'Oh, don't get into all of that again, please!' Millicent said. 'Can't we have a few minutes to digest our meals?'

Trinity had a few questions and a few comments to make, but they would likely do nothing more than earn him contempt from Earl Bates and Vincent Battles. He continued to eat in silence.

After everyone had finished eating, Trinity rose and followed Holly into her father's study. 'I'm going to look the books over again,' Holly told him, nodding toward the blue-bound ledgers on her father's desk.

'Is the Owl in serious trouble?'

'We've been in better shape,' she smiled, 'but things will be much better once we get the herd to Fort Bridger.' Beneath her smile, Holly still wore a look of concern. He could say nothing to comfort her.

'If you'd just show me where my room is, I'll turn in early,' Trinity said.

'The men will be staying up by the fire, drinking coffee and brandy. You're welcome to . . . '

'I don't really think that's a good idea, do you?' Trinity wondered what sort of fuel the brandy would add to the fiery disagreement between Vincent Battles and Earl Bates.

'I suppose not,' she admitted. 'Come along then, and I'll get you settled.'

Climbing the staircase they reached the upper floor, Trinity walking behind Holly. There were six doors off the corridor. He assumed that some of the doors led to the bedrooms of Holly and her sister. One of the others must belong to Russell. Certainly one had been used by Earl Bates — probably his boyhood room.

Holly seemed to see the thoughts behind Trinity's eyes. 'Don't worry,' she said with a short laugh. 'I'm not putting you in with Vincent — he said he prefers to sleep on the leather couch downstairs.'

At the very end of the hall, Holly stood beside a door and swung it open. A breath of stale air met them. The room did not smell exactly musty, but of disuse.

'This used to be my mother's sewing room,' Holly told him, lighting a match to place to the wick in the bedside lamp. 'There's a bed, and little else, I'm afraid.'

'That's about all I usually require while I'm sleeping,' Trinity grinned.

'You're an easy man to satisfy,' Holly said, her golden eyes glittering in the lamplight.

'Most always,' he said, feeling oddly uncomfortable being alone with her in the room. Their eyes met and held for a few moments longer than necessary, then Holly turned hers away pointedly. Why? Because she was Vincent Battles's intended? He had never asked her directly about that, although everyone on the Owl seemed to be taking it for granted.

'I'll send Tonio up with bed linen,' Holly said. That was a luxury Trinity was unaccustomed to. 'Will I see you at the breakfast table?'

'I doubt it,' he answered. 'I've been told I'd better make myself useful around here, so I'll be riding out early.'

'Where?'

'Probably up to Dos Picos. I gather that they still haven't combed all the strays out of those canyons.' He paused and said quietly, 'There's no point in telling anyone else that's where I've gone, Holly.'

'No, I won't,' she answered hesitantly. What was he holding back from her? 'Not if you don't want me to. I'll have Alicia make you a few ham sandwiches to take with you. She'll leave them out. And there's always coffee on.'

Trinity nodded his thanks and Holly went out, her boot heels clicking on the wood of the corridor floor. Trinity looked around the small room and began unbuttoning his faded blue shirt. He bent to look out the window which overlooked the bunkhouse area. It seemed relatively quiet over there; perhaps Vincent Battles and Earl had somehow managed to restore order.

Approaching sounds turned Trinity's head. It was Tonio with folded sheets and a pillowcase across his arm. Entering, the boy tossed the linen down on the bare mattress of the bed.

'Looks like you're settling in pretty well, Trinity,' Tonio commented.

'It's all illusion, my friend,' Trinity told him.

'What?' Tonio had not understood the remark.

'I mean that I won't be around much longer,' Trinity said. Tonio appeared to be disappointed. 'Too bad — I will miss having someone here who I can talk to.'

'You've always got the horses, Tonio,' Trinity said with a warm smile. 'And they're probably better listeners than I am.'

Tonio's smile was like quicksilver, there and then gone. 'Yes, that is right. I always have the horses.' *If nothing else*, he seemed to add silently.

Trinity slept soundly, with only one moment of interruption. He was awakened by the sound of boot heels clicking down the corridor. He considered the sound and lent it no weight. After all, Russell and Earl must climb the stairs and enter their rooms sometime. Nevertheless, he swung his feet to the floor, scratched at his rumpled hair and went to the door of his room. A lifetime of caution caused him to open the door a bare inch and look out. It was difficult to tell in the poor light, but the man standing in front of a door along the corridor, looked like Vincent Battles.

When the door opened, Trinity saw an arm dressed in some flimsy fabric reach out and take the shadow's hand, leading him into the room.

Trinity frowned, but it was none of his business if Battles visited Millicent, no matter the time of day or night.

★　★　★

With the dawn, Trinity rose from his comfortable bed. It was a dark, bleak dawn. There was no color in the sky, as Trinity saw when he peered out the window of his room. Black storm clouds had settled in across the Owl and silver beads of rain, slanted across the sky, struck the glass of the window and rivuleted away.

He dressed quickly and crept down the stairs, wanting to make his way out before anyone else was stirring. A sleeping form on the couch in front of the cold fireplace surprised him briefly before he recalled Holly saying that Vincent Battles preferred to sleep there. He crept past the Owl foreman, not wanting to answer any questions.

In the kitchen, the dimmest of possible lights glowed. There was a fire in the iron stove that had burned down to no more than a fist-sized collection of glowing coals. He knew the fire could be easily prodded to life, but he had no intention of doing so.

Touching the blue enamel coffee pot resting on top of the stove, he found it still hot and helped himself to a cup.

On the nearby counter, as Holly had promised, sat two ham sandwiches wrapped in waxed paper and then in oilskin. These he scooped up and shoved into his coat pocket. Drinking his coffee quickly, he watched out the kitchen window, hoping that no one was yet stirring — but someone was up and busy in the bunkhouse. A lantern glowed there. Probably it was only Cooky busy in his kitchen.

Nevertheless Trinity felt some urgency about his mission. Thunder boomed close at hand and the rain began to fall more heavily. Placing his cup aside he went out into the cold darkness and made his way toward the stable.

The place was as dark as sin. He fumbled around, finding the lantern on the wall where he remembered it hanging, struck a match and brought it to life. By the feeble glow he walked the length of the stalls toward his horse. Other animals watched, some of them as if eager to travel, others sleepy-eyed, wondering why this human had chosen to intrude on their slumber.

The piebald seemed neither sleepy nor eager to be moving. Perhaps it had heard the thunder, seen lightning flashes, and knew that it would be a bad day on the trail. Trinity had the same feeling, and with even more reason.

'It's got to be done,' he murmured to the spotted horse as he saddled it and slipped the piebald its bit. From his saddle-bags Trinity recovered his rolled-up slicker and donned it before leading his horse into the gray-black darkness of the stormy dawn.

He rode directly west, the sky colored with reflected dawn light between ragged silver clouds. At times lightning and thunder rumbled and slashed brilliant white against the black, clotted northern skies. Once a shaft of low sunlight pierced through the darkness, lighting the thick grass of the plains, illuminating the silver rain and the far hills, but it was quickly smothered again by the gathered clouds.

Trinity rode on, his head bowed against the wind and the slap of driven rain. No one, he thought, had seen him leave, but in this weather there could be a hundred men around him and he wouldn't have known it.

By retracing the route he and Holly had ridden, he was able to set his course toward Dos Picos with some certainty. An hour later he found himself entering the mouth of one of the tangled canyons in the notorious stretch of badlands, riding upward into the rugged hills. The rain had eased up slightly; the sky was a little brighter. The winds, however, came howling down the canyons, setting the brush alongside the trail to a violent tremble. Despite the fact that the trail was awash with red mud, he could make out horse tracks here and there, both coming and going from the wild country.

It did not escape his notice that there were no cattle prints to be seen. None! Supposedly the cowboys from the Owl had been riding up into this country each day, hieing out the lost or strayed cattle. Trinity frowned. If they had been doing so, they had been carrying the steers on their backs.

He continued on his way, riding upslope into the face of the rushing wind which whistled eerily through the sagebrush and battered the limbs of the occasional pinyon pine tree he passed. The rain fell steadily, at times in a driving rush which hammered his shoulders and veiled the trail ahead, at times gently if still persistent, allowing him a view of his chosen path. He could now see the crest of the trail. A rocky outcropping like some ancient sentinel towered against the rainy skies as it had for centuries. At times when the rain closed off his vision, he had now only to keep the craggy bluff on his right shoulder to keep to the meandering trail.

Topping out the grade, Trinity slowed his piebald which he could now feel was laboring beneath him. At the ridge, Trinity halted the horse and gave it time to blow. He could feel the animal shuddering under him and apologized mentally to it for bringing it out in this weather, over this ground.

From the crown of the trail he looked down through the drifting clouds on to the valley below, trying to find an easy path down. He also turned in his saddle to look back, reassuring himself that no man was following him. Clouds wove together and spun themselves across the canyon like gray ghosts. From the higher dark clouds the rain continued to stream down. Trinity took the time to eat one of the ham sandwiches — while his horse rested — before starting down, riding through the low silver clouds as the wind pummeled him. The air was ripe with the scent of sage, fresh with the smell of new rain. The day was cold, still tumultuous and windy, but the skies had brightened to a dull steel color.

He found the flats half an hour on and began riding over the grasslands, his horse up to its hocks in places in cold standing water. He rode more slowly now, his slicker open, the flap of his coat folded back for easier access to his Colt. He continued on without illusions. There were men out here who would kill him for intruding on their secret domain.

Half an hour on, he found what he had been looking for.

7

The dark herd was bunched against the weather, using each other's bodies for warmth. Lightning flared up against the sky as thunder rumbled across the meadow. In this weather someone was certain to be riding herd to quell any threat of a stampede. The close strike of lightning or the unexpected roar of thunder could set the skittish herd to running.

Trinity kept his eyes moving as he rose. It was difficult to see much through the mesh of falling rain, but then it would be difficult for an Owl rider to identify Trinity — he would be just another mounted man, in the confusing shadows of the storm.

He approached the herd steadily. He already had most of the answers he needed. *Who* was obvious — Vincent Battles, not Earl Bates, had been on the scene when the old foreman, Dalton Remy, had been strung up. It was Battles who had brought his own men in and dismissed many of the longtime Owl riders. Remy, of course, had to be gotten out of the way — probably he or his men had come across the second herd. At any rate, Vincent Battles meant to take his place. Why was also obvious — simply, Battles was here to make some money for himself. A lot of money. He had nothing to fear if the plan failed; Owl would take all of the blame. *How* Battles meant to do all of this had troubled Trinity for a while, until Tonio told him about the *other* herd. This herd.

Trinity now began to ride among the cattle. He saw many of the obvious symptoms. They had excessive discharges from their nostrils. They looked at him lethargically with rheumy eyes. He ran his hand across the back of one of the steers, feeling lesions in the hide, and the suppurations left from tick bites.

They had Texas fever.

Probably the herd had been purchased in Mexico for pennies on the dollar compared to what healthy steers would bring, and driven north to be hidden in this valley near the Owl range. The army would find itself in a bind when these cattle were driven into Fort Bridger. Their own examining officer had checked the herd — the real Owl herd — and certified it. The replacement herd couldn't have even withstood a casual examination.

The point was that the army had already contracted for Owl beef. That could not just be ignored. There would be big trouble for this Lieutenant Ross who had signed the contract, for the base commander. Beyond the army's own need for beef, Trinity had been told that a part of the herd was intended for the settled Indians, as a part of the price they received to refrain from hostilities. They certainly would not accept these animals; the army would lose any good faith it may have purchased.

Which was why First Lieutenant Trinity Ray Tucker of the army procurement office was here. Suspicions had been raised. From what Trinity knew of it, a few of the riders dismissed by Vincent Battles had done some complaining at Fort Bridger and expressed doubts. Perhaps they had run across a mis-branded steer or the entire hidden herd themselves while actually working the Dos Picos country for strays.

Vincent Battles's suspicion had been correct — Trinity had hardly met Russell Bates by accident back along the North Platte. Trinity was aware that the young man was AWOL, knew that Russell was heir to the Owl Ranch, and that there was possible trouble down that way. Falling in with Russell gave him entrée where he would have had difficulty otherwise explaining his presence on the ranch.

Trinity swung down from his piebald now and examined some of the handiwork that had also puzzled him until recently. He was used to men re-working cattle brands, changing them to their own, but he thought that this was the first time he had ever seen a brand changed to match its genuine owner's.

The brand on the hip of the red steer he stood beside now had been altered, but was not quite perfect. Squinting through the rain, Trinity saw enough to make it all come clear. The small loops of iron that he had found in the smith's shed had indeed been broken off of a genuine Owl brand. The eyes removed, leaving only the shape of the head for an iron. Turning the broken pieces, Trinity had managed to make a known brand of them. The loops placed back to back formed a 'CC' brand, with the first 'C' reversed. It was a known brand out of New Mexico, owned by five men.

Cinco Compadres, or 'five friends' was the proper way to read the Double C brand. All of these cattle had been sold off by the CC, knowing that they would never be able to market them, that all were diseased. They had probably been grateful when Battles took them away for a tiny fraction of their healthy worth. He must have seemed like a madman, but Vincent Battles had a plan in mind. He had worked for the Owl before and it must have occurred to him that the butted Cs looked enough like the eyes of the Owl brand that it would take no artistic running iron work to burn an authentic-looking Owl on the steers. Especially if the original Owl head outline could be used.

Trinity checked another brand. This one was slightly misaligned so that the eyes obviously were not on the same iron as the one used for the outline. There was a gap between the eyes and the head where there should not have been. Two irons had been used then, the original CC back to back iron and the existing Owl outline.

Vincent Battles must have already been driving this herd into the hidden valley before Holly ever sent for him. With her old foreman — Dalton Remy

— missing, she had needed help. Battles knew that she was more or less alone on the Owl, with Earl in Texas and Russell in the army. He arrived a few days after being summoned, bringing his own men, probably seeming to be some sort of savior knight to Holly — when all he had meant to do was profit from her.

What did he care if the Owl went broke? The army would certainly never do business with it again once these infected cattle were delivered. But Vincent Battles would have pocketed his profits and gone on his way. No wonder Battles had been upset by Russell's unexpected arrival and nearly furious when Earl Bates returned. Battles probably cursed the old man, Lew Bates, for having the temerity to die on him just when Vincent seemingly had things well in hand, and making it necessary to notify Earl Bates. Holly was out of her depth and knew it. All Battles had to do was convince her to stay at home, drive the infected herd through to Bridger and demand payment for the herd which had already been declared healthy and contracted for. That would take a lot of cool nerve, but Vincent Battles was not short on that commodity.

He could not now let Earl Bates, especially, go along on the drive. Earl was an experienced cattleman and would immediately know that these beeves were not an Owl herd. Hence the furious argument between Earl and Battles. It was not over leadership, but because Vincent Battles knew his herd could not stand up under scrutiny. Battles was probably already laying plans for the murder of Earl and Russell along the trail. He had to — his position was desperate now.

And Holly?

She had expressed her determination to travel with the herd to Fort Bridger, and could not be allowed to.

Trinity had seen enough. He had to get back to the Owl and warn Holly and Russell what was happening.

Trinity knew now why his father had sent for Russell, what was important enough to summon him back from his army service. Somehow Lew Bates had found out the truth. Maybe Dalton Remy had gone to tell the old man what he had discovered before he was murdered.

Trinity turned the piebald eastward, toward the crooked trail over Dos Picos. The clouds had thinned just enough in the east that the sun now appeared as a misty red ball over the twin peaks. The brush beside the trail was soaked with rain water, glinting briefly in the moment of captured sunlight, the trail itself sodden, making for heavy going. Trinity let the piebald pick its own way.

The pain in his back was swift and searing, striking out of nowhere. Then the rolling echo of the distant rifle shot reached Trinity's ears. He was already falling from the saddle of the startled horse when the sound reached his ears. Whoever it was taking the shot, he was a better marksman than the ambusher of the previous day.

Trinity had been struck just below his smallest rib by a man using a heavy-bore rifle. He felt the hot seep of his blood as he landed sprawled against the cold, sodden earth. The thorny mesquite where he landed ripped at his cheek and hand. His horse was gone, clever animal. Another shot clipped brush above him, encouraging Trinity to offer no target to the rifleman. He kept low, scrabbling and clawing his way toward a depression on the hillside.

He had gotten careless — spending too much time down among the herd of cattle, when his first glimpse of the steers had been enough to tell him all that he needed to know. Now he had to pay for that lapse in judgement — the men behind him could not afford to let him live. If he were to reach the Owl and reveal the plans of the riders and their masquerading steers, their hopes of a big payday would be lost.

The air was cool and water-heavy

when he breathed in. This portion of the peaks must have burned off not long ago, for his body was covered from head to toe with damp ash. His side was fiery, flaring. He rolled into the depression when he reached it and took the time and trouble to peel back his shirt and survey the damage.

Clean through, the shot had gone, tearing away muscle and hide, but missing bone and any vital organ. That lifted his spirits somewhat, but the blood still flowed freely and the pain did not abate. He could congratulate himself for not being dead, but dead would not have hurt so much.

Tearing a strip from the bottom of his shirt he made a bandage, which he strapped tightly around his torso. Then he buttoned his still-smoldering jacket again, closed his slicker, and lay shivering in the sink as ragged clouds drifted overhead, seeming determined to reunite into thunderheads.

The day continued, gray and time-less, the wind curled its rattling way through the sheltering brush; his side continued to burn; his damaged kidneys, suffered in the bunkhouse fight with Willie Meese, decided to kick in with their share of torment. Probably they had been jarred loose again in his fall from the horse, just as they had begun to heal.

Now what?

He had to move, to rise and get out of there, or eventually he would be discovered. His attacker could not afford to let him slip away. Yet by rising he would offer a target to the rifleman who had undoubtedly followed and would be much nearer now. If he had his horse . . . but he did not, the animal, in an urge toward self-preservation, had run off. Trinity's eyes lifted to the shattered bulk of the twin peaks beyond, knowing he could not scale them by clawing his way across the earth. Regaining the trail was an even worse choice. The rifleman, his pursuers, would be watching the trail for him to emerge.

He had to move! So long as he was

moving, so long as the Colt revolver on his hip retained its snap and bite, there was a chance for survival. There was none if he lay cowering in the depression like a wounded animal.

Trinity got to all fours and peered up through the screen of brush surrounding him — a tangle of sumac, twisted manzanita, greasewood and sage. His first glimpse gave him a view of a horse's legs — a red roan — as it was walked slowly up the canyon road. Its rider was undoubtedly searching from side to side, looking for what he knew had to be a wounded man. Trinity could see the cool glint of a rifle barrel's metal where it dangled loosely from the rider's hand. It was now or never, he thought.

Taking a desperate gamble, Trinity took aim through the scrub forest of brush at the shadowy figure of the rider. The close explosion of the .44 Colt racketed away as the rider flung his rifle aside and fell from his bucking horse. Trinity scrambled painfully to his feet and dashed toward the horse like a staggering avenger, revolver in his hand.

He found the horse standing trembling along the path, then let his eyes scour the brush beside the road until they found the man sprawled in the mud there, soot on his narrow face.

'You . . .' Willie Meese screamed and he grabbed for the rifle on the muddy earth beside him.

Trinity shot him before his hand could grasp the Winchester. He walked toward the man across the uneven, rocky ground, holding his side with one hand. Willie looked up with haunted eyes. Rain fell into his face. His nose was covered with a sooty and mud-flecked bandage still. His lips barely moved as he gasped his last words, 'I knew you were trouble, Trinity . . .'

Then his chest deflated and Willie lay staring, unseeing, at the iron sky which had mended itself once more and formed a sunless, rainy whole.

Trinity picked up Meese's rifle, gathered the reins to the frightened red roan and levered himself into the saddle, his eyes on his backtrail, knowing that Willie Meese could not have been out here on the hunt alone. He had to get back to the Owl. He had to warn them all, had to get his side bandaged properly before he died on the cold and lonely trail. He started the roan up the slope, the going sloppy underfoot as the rain continued to cascade down. His entire body was shaking with cold except for his side which continued to flare with unremitting fire.

He rode on, upward, the roan slipping on the muddy surface which overlay smooth rock. Trinity wondered inconsequentially where the piebald had run off to. He would have to give that horse some further training.

If he ever saw it again.

The sun broke through the grayness, blindingly bright in his eyes. Along the trail, and beside it, all along the hillslope small pools of water reflected like brilliant mirrors. Then the sun was

133

gone, as quickly as it had appeared as the dark clouds merged again, fighting back against the sunlight. Gloom and shadow reigned once more as Trinity crested the trail. He sat panting, aching; the horse under him heaved with exertion. He placed his hand on the roan's neck, stroking it, thanking it for its effort.

The three men rounded a bend in the trail and were suddenly before him, rifles unsheathed, horses frothing. He could not identify their faces at this distance, but they seemed to know who he was although the rain swirled and he was seated on Willie Meese's horse. The first bullet whipped past his ear, so near that — had he been a pirate — he would have lost his earring. Meese's rifle had been left behind, and Trinity's was lost, the piebald carrying it away when it ran.

He slicked his Colt revolver from its damp holster and fired back twice at the savage men. That did nothing to slow their uphill charge although one of them slapped at his shoulder as if bee-stung. Aiming was uncertain, the horse unsteady beneath him, the sky dark and constantly shifting.

Trinity knew he did not wish to go to ground again, not with three riflemen pursuing him and so he heeled the roan roughly and started away at a leaping, head jarring pace into the depths of another feeder canyon with no obvious trail. The brush was heavy, thorny and prickly. Mesquite and nopal cactus grew heavily in the bottom which was gray granite glossed with run-off water. Rifle shots followed him, bullets scything through brush and ricocheting violently off a rock face dangerously near to his head. He plunged ahead, driving the sturdy roan down the canyon which led — Trinity did not know where it led, only that he was going away from the hunters on some mad dash through thorny underbrush.

These were the thickets that Owl cattle were known to hide in, to escape to, to get lost in. The roan was a good little horse, but it was unused to brush-popping unlike those Texas-bred horses Trinity had once ridden down in the Big Thicket country on another, long ago mission for the army.

His head jolted back on his neck as the roan, urged to run too fast along the watercourse came to a hard stop, bracing its front legs. Trinity held up for a moment, as much for himself as for the roan. He could see no one behind him, hear no one rushing through the brush in pursuit. Maybe they had given up — or perhaps they knew that this canyon led nowhere at all.

There was no choice, Trinity started on. The swift water flowed past under the horse's feet, washing the stone floor of the canyon free of debris and mud. The gray walls of the chute, through which he now rode, rose up high against the murky sky. Somehow the cold wind still blew strongly enough to buffet him, channeled down the canyon by the force of the fitful storm. He could see no way up and out of the stony canyon, nothing ahead of him that promised an escape.

He let the horse pick its way more slowly. If it were to break a leg, his situation would become desperate. Even without the bullet wound he would have been sorely pressed to walk out of this tangle, find his way down the slopes and hike to the Owl.

He found himself thinking not so much of guiding the horse now, but of those on the Owl who were about to be ruined, very probably killed before Vincent Battles's game was played out. Russell was a good kid, but Trinity doubted he could stand up to Battles and whatever men he took along with him to finish sealing his scheme. Earl Bates, a man Trinity did not particularly like, but who was his most capable ally, would certainly be gunned down.

And Holly? Trinity thought of the red-headed girl with the hot temper and golden eyes, and knew he could not allow anything to happen to her.

Millicent, Trinity believed, would

always find a way to survive — the meeting he had witnessed last night between her and Vincent Battles now had him nearly convinced that she was hardly an innocent.

The canyon had narrowed down to form a stony wedge. As it did, the cold running water grew deeper and the roan, not liking it, grew balky. The onrushing charge in the thicket beyond the rampaging creek caused Trinity to rein in hard and draw his pistol. Dark-eyed fury studied him, challenged him. The longhorn steer had somehow managed to entrap its horns in the thick, tangled manzanita wood. It was furious, twisting its head this way and that, rattling the brush with its six-foot horns as it tried futilely to free itself. On the best of days it would have been a hazardous undertaking to try to help the steer free itself. This was far from the best of days. There was nothing Trinity could do but ride on, hoping that the longhorn had enough retained strength to eventually break free of the woody manzanita.

The rain fell, much harder now — the way before Trinity was screened by it. He was sore, his wound throbbed, his kidneys ached. He was hungry and searched his pockets for the other ham sandwich he had been carrying, not caring what sort of shape it might be in — but he had lost it somewhere along the way.

The stony chute ended suddenly. He had to thank the roan for having the sense to stop. The water from the canyon formed itself into a waterfall which sheeted out and fanned downward across a sheer stone face. Trinity backed the shuddering red roan carefully away from the rim of the falls.

Now what? He could not go back, could not go forward, and the men with the rifles were somewhere on the trail behind, stalking him.

8

The hard rain stung Trinity's face and the cold wind gusted as if it would thrust him over the ledge to plummet down the waterfall. He backed the red roan a few more steps. The cautious animal was eager to obey — it liked none of this and probably wondered what the creature on his back was thinking of, taking him down this terrible trail.

There was only one possibility, of course, to somehow clamber up the side of the canyon to the flats above. The slope was red mud over gray granite, exceedingly slippery and dangerously steep. Even if he could crawl up it somehow, what was to be done with the horse? Trinity thought of stripping its gear and sending it back in the direction they had come from, but that would leave him afoot again out in the dangerous wilds.

Studying the hillside through the driving rain, he thought he could make out a possible route up the slope. He would have to dismount and lead the horse, but then if the horse slid back and he were still holding the reins, they both would plunge to the bottom of the canyon. Still, it had to be tried.

There was no choice.

'Sorry, friend,' he muttered to the worried roan horse, 'but we've got to do this.'

Stepping down from the horse into the cold, rushing water, Trinity gathered the reins and started on his way. The horse balked, and Trinity could not blame it. At least Trinity had fingers capable of clawing his way up the treacherous slope. It would be something of a miracle if the hoofed animal could make the climb. He started on.

He made his way ten feet up the crumbling, drenched path — if it could be termed that — and parked himself on a narrow ledge of cold stone, the rain coursing past beneath him. He tugged at the roan's tether, watched the fear in the animal's eyes and its first faltering attempt at finding purchase in order to follow.

The horse's hoofs alternately clattered off stone and were sucked down into the mud, but after two hesitant starts it managed to traverse the distance to stand, shuddering, beside Trinity on the narrow ledge. Feeling some confidence now, Trinity started up the hill slope again, the reins to the roan wrapped tightly around one wrist. He was clambering over a cold, muddy projection some three feet high when he felt his arm whipped back.

The horse was falling away from him. There was one brief moment when Trinity thought of whipping the reins free of his wrist, but he clung to the rocky projection, gritted his teeth and cursed, prayed, or both. The roan found its footing in some way and scrambled upward, going nearly to its chest in the attempt. It stood over Trinity, its heated breath washing down over him. Again they rested. Again Trinity rose — not looking down at the bottom of the stony chute, but upward toward the rain-veiled rimrock.

He had only begun. The episode was repeated half a dozen to a dozen times as they ascended. Finally Trinity rolled over on to the flat ground that had seemed so far above and lay on his back in the muddy water, against cold stone, breathing in gasps, the rain falling on to his face. The horse scrambled up and over and Trinity watched the roan with unchecked admiration.

'You're a good old boy,' Trinity said. 'Willie Meese never deserved you.'

He led the horse across the flat ground for a way, looking for a way down — if one there was. Trinity found himself standing on what seemed to be the end of the earth, the sky dark and tumbling overhead, the land below hidden by scudding gray clouds. Lightning flared up, far to the north, followed by the shallow rumbling of distant thunder.

Walking on, moving slowly and with extreme caution, he saw what seemed to be a path running along the very edge of the bluff where he had marooned himself. Pencil thin, it meandered along the rugged rim of the bluff. It seemed to be broken away in places, nearly invisible in others where encroaching brush had overgrown it.

He knew what he was looking at. It was an ancient Indian trail, its former path narrowed by weather and the passage of time. A few hundred years ago — eons ago, one could be sure — this trail had led up and across the plateau to some camp, ceremonial site or hunting place. Then, it had been well-traveled and safe to follow. Now it was neither; it lay crumbling away on the uncertain edge of the plateau. Still, Trinity was somewhat buoyed by this discovery.

The trail had been used for a purpose — to reach the high country, perhaps to find safety when the Indians felt threatened on the valley below. He could no longer follow this remnant of a path, but by riding parallel to it, he was certain he could find his way down the Dos Picas. The trail ended somewhere; it had begun somewhere.

Feeling a little relieved, he swung on to the cold section of the rain-slick saddle and turned the weary roan's head northward.

By keeping the ancient trail in sight at all times, he could follow its course and also use it as a warning should he ride perilously close to the edge of the bluff. The wind continued to howl from the north, the driven rain stinging his eyes. Committed now, Trinity rode doggedly on. The land dipped a little and rose a little, but it remained relatively flat as he wove his way across.

Abruptly the slope of the land increased, and he held the horse up and tried again to search through the uncertain weather for his course. Down, the path was going down toward its presumed terminus on the valley floor below. He rode with more confidence now although the going was no easier. The horse labored beneath him, but traveled gamely on.

There was a brief clearing of the skies and sunlight shafted down, allowing Trinity to see the valley where the Owl herd stood. Steam rose from their dark, huddled bodies.

At the end of another miserably cold hour, his clothing wet through, sticking to him like paste despite the torn slicker he was wearing, he found himself riding free and easy across the long valley of the Owl Ranch.

★ ★ ★

Tonio looked up from his work with wide, startled eyes as the horseman in dark silhouette rode in through the stable doors. Beyond the lone rider, lightning carved the long skies into tumult and the rain continued to fall — now thinly, but colder than ever.

Tonio recognized the horse, of course — he was familiar with them all. The red roan was Willie Meese's mount, and just now it was rain-streaked and weary looking. It staggered on a bit as it entered its warm, welcome home.

'Hello, Tonio,' Trinity said, stepping down from the saddle. He, too, staggered a little as he walked toward the nearby partition and clung to it, his head spinning.

'Hello, Lieutenant!' Tonio said excitedly. Trinity frowned.

'How'd you find out about me?' he asked.

'It was when your horse came back. He's fine, right over there,' Tonio said, jabbing a thumb in the direction of the piebald. 'Some of the men saw it come in riderless and they came over here. That man named Plimford — you know him?'

'We've met,' Trinity answered. His legs were unsteady under him, trembling with the cold and with blood loss.

'Him and a man he called Rush came in and asked me what happened. Of course, I didn't know — what could I say? They went and got your saddlebags off the piebald and opened them up. They found some sort of papers that had your name and rank.'

'Have you told anyone else, Tonio?' Trinity wanted to know.

'No, sir. I didn't know what I should do. Plimford and Rush, they didn't want to tell anyone either. Plimford he says, 'Well it looks like the boys took care of him. I guess it doesn't matter now.' Rush, he says, 'It might make more trouble with the army for us. Best we forget the whole thing.' Then they stuffed the papers back in your saddle-bags and left.'

'I don't suppose it makes much difference now,' Trinity said. His side was still burning with pain and he was weak in the knees. Tonio noticed it.

'Did you get hurt, Trinity?'

'I got nudged a little by some lead.'

'Shot? Where?' Tonio asked with concern.

'Just creased my side, but I need to have it tended to.'

'Sure,' the kid replied. 'You go talk to my mother. She acts gruff, mostly because she's tired all the time, but she'll take care of you.'

Trinity frowned. 'Who else is in the house, Tonio?'

'Just her — and Miss Millicent. She don't hardly ever go anywhere.'

Trinity's puzzlement deepened. 'But where are the others? Russell Bates and Earl. Holly?'

'They rode out,' Tonio said. 'With all of the Texans. I heard Earl Bates say the hell with Vincent Battles. Said he had time to bunch the trail herd, then when the rain lets up, they would start the drive right now — not when Battles got ready to.'

It would take some work sorting the herd in this rain, but Earl was right — by the time the rain let up, which looked to be in early afternoon, he would be able to start his drive. But where was Battles? All of his men? He asked Tonio.

'I don't know. Battles rode out even before they did. It looked like he had most of his crew with him. Look

149

around, Trinity, there ain't but half a dozen horses left here.'

He was right. Besides the piebald, Meese's red roan and the army bay Russell Bates had ridden in on, there were only a handful of other horses in the barn. He thought he knew where Battles had gone. Having learned of Earl Bates's decision to start the Owl herd on its way, he had ridden off toward the counterfeit herd to try to get an earlier start. That was as far as his thinking went before a swirling confusion swept through his mind. He had to get his wound attended to and now, or else he was going to be no further help to himself or anyone else. Tonio, his face drawn with concern, encouraged Trinity: 'Go see my mother. She will know what to do, and it seems most of her work must be finished for the day with everyone gone.'

'You're right, Tonio. Thanks, I'll see her.'

If he could make it that far. The rain was drifting down lightly; the gusting wind continued to twist it into sheer veils. There was water standing in the muddy yard between barn and house — and the house seemed miles away.

He stumbled out into the rain, holding his side, keeping his eyes turned down away from the force of the wind-blown rain. His boots slipped on the muddy earth and he stepped twice into ankle-deep puddles of cold water. He took one step at a time, drawn along by the feeble glow of light ahead which promised warmth and care.

Using the handrail, he pulled himself up the wooden steps on to the back porch and slipped into the incredible warmth of the kitchen. Alicia was at the sink, paring knife in her hand. She turned, her eyes startled and annoyed with the interruption. She immediately took in Trinity's condition, put her knife aside, muttered *madre de Dios*, and came to where Trinity stood, weaving and shuddering, wiping her hands on her apron.

'Don't stand there — sit down,'

Alicia said, 'are you a crazy man?'

Thankfully, Trinity sagged on to one of the wooden kitchen chairs. Alicia, muttering under her breath, helped him tug off his slicker and sodden jacket. Trinity winced as her fingers pulled up his shirt to find the muddy, bloody makeshift bandage beneath it.

She tried to work tenderly, but separating the filthy bandage from the scabbed wound drove a searing spike of pain through Trinity. He thought for a moment he would pass out from it. Perhaps he did — for a moment later he could hear the tea kettle whistling and found himself shirtless as Alicia, her breath exhaling in tiny puffs, worked on the bullet wound with a pan of hot water and a cloth. She then applied some kind of poultice to the bullet hole, back and front. Whatever it was smelled like mustard and burned like it. But after only a few seconds the heat disappeared and Alicia began wrapping a clean bandage around him as he stood bare-chested before her.

'I can't do much for the other scrapes and bruises,' she told him, 'but they will heal on their own.'

'I thank you for what you've done,' Trinity said.

The inner door opened behind Trinity, and he flinched and reached for his holstered gun. A somehow familiar scent reached him and he turned to see the graceful cat that was Millicent Bates in the doorway. She held a teacup and saucer and wore an amused smile.

'I heard the kettle singing,' she told Alicia, 'and it reminded me that I would like another cup of tea.'

'In one minute,' Alicia said with controlled anger. To Trinity, Millicent said: 'They shot you again, did they? If I were you I wouldn't go out riding if every time I went someone tried to kill me.' She bent low, her dark feline eyes narrowing. 'Who was it this time?'

'I couldn't tell you which one of them it was. Meese, probably.'

'Well, you made it back again, didn't you. This time,' Millicent said. Now her purr of a voice sounded more like a soft growl. She accepted a cup of tea from Alicia and swept out of the room, the hem of her dark dress whispering against the floor-boards.

'Is she the only one home?' Trinity asked.

'Yes, the only one.' Alicia's mouth tightened as she said it.

Trinity was standing, his fresh bandage already showing a spot of crimson blood. He picked his dirty shirt up from the chair where it had been thrown. Alicia's eyes narrowed.

'Where you going?'

'After the herd — I have to catch up with it.'

'In the shape you are in? You are a crazy man,' she said, wagging her head. 'Wait, and I'll find you a new shirt, maybe a dry coat. Dalton Remy, he left some of his clothes in the closet, if they still are there.'

Trinity waited, watching the light rain fall beyond the kitchen window. His side continued to ache; he still felt a little light-headed, but he had to catch up with the Owl herd because he knew what Vincent Battles was going to do.

Alicia returned with a heavy blue flannel shirt and a cracked leather jacket. She helped him to dress. The clothes fitted reasonably well. At least they were dry.

'There wasn't a hat, I don't suppose,' he asked.

'There was, but I didn't think . . . wait, I'll get it,' she said, bustling away into the interior of the house. The hat was a little large for him, but it was better than none at all. Thanking Alicia profusely, he went back out into the gray of the day, her dark eyes following him doubtfully.

Tonio was still in the barn, fussing with the red roan when Trinity walked in. 'You riding out again?' Tonio asked, his own doubt showing in his eyes.

'Have to, Tonio. Would you fit that bay horse with my gear?' Trinity had the feeling that hoisting his own saddle would probably tear the wound in his side open.

'Sure, I'll do it. The army bay, not the piebald?'

'No, the bay will do. My horse has had a rough morning. I need a fresh animal under me.'

'That horse hasn't been ridden since Mister Russell came in on him.'

'He should be ready to go then,' Trinity said. Tonio remained dubious. 'It's all right, Tonio. The bay and I are both property of the US Army.'

The sun was sporadic but bright as it shined through the clouds hovering over the long grass meadow where only a small remnant of the Owl herd remained. Glancing at the sky, Trinity figured that Earl Bates had guessed right about the storm breaking up. Earl had lived most of his life in this part of the country and probably knew the weather patterns better than most.

The cattle left behind in the valley raised languid eyes to him, perhaps wondering what was going to happen to them now that the other cattle had been driven off the meadow. Probably not unlike horses, Trinity had never met a cow that exhibited much more intelligence than it took to stand in the rain and mow grass.

He hit the trail. It was simple to follow after the herd. A hundred and fifty steers leave a broad path in their passing. Where they had not trodden, the long grass sparkled where the sun struck as with chips of diamond, ruby and topaz. The skies continued to clear. Only occasionally would a light spate of rain fall — the storm's parting, contemptuous gesture.

Riding unencumbered, Trinity had no doubt he would quickly catch up with the trail herd. He only hoped it would be soon enough. There was a lot at stake and a lot of men's lives hung in the balance.

9

Earl Bates didn't seem too pleased to see Trinity when he found the man riding drag, following the Owl herd northward. Bates eyed the horse with the US brand on its flank and then growled a welcome.

'I see you made it, Lieutenant.'

'How'd you find out?' Trinity asked, slowing his horse a little to keep pace with the tall blue roan Bates straddled.

'Everyone knows by now. One man tells another, and soon it's common knowledge. I suppose I should have guessed it earlier — everyone knew you were more than you pretended to be.' Bates paused to use his coiled lariat to hie a lagging steer toward the herd. When he returned, his scowl was still in place.

'What's so urgent that you felt the need to catch up with us, Lieutenant, even wounded as you are?'

'Does it show?' Trinity asked with a weak grin.

'Man, you should see the way you're sitting on your saddle — yes, it shows. Now what's the emergency?'

Trinity told Bates as briefly as he could what Vincent Battles and his men had been up to, how he had found the CC herd. Bates listened, his scowl deepening. 'I knew Battles was up to no good from the first,' Earl Bates muttered.

'This valley where I found his herd of sick cattle . . . does it have a name?'

'We call it Bear Valley. My father once thought of buying it, but I talked him out of it. The Dos Picos breaks up the property too much to manage properly although there's good grass and water over there.'

'Well,' Trinity continued, 'Bear Valley then — is there a trail out of there?'

'Sure,' Earl said. 'South Pass. That's the way they must have brought the cattle in. But leaving that way, it's a much longer route to get to Fort Bridger — if you're suggesting that's still their intention.'

'No, I'm not,' Trinity said. 'I just mean, if there's not a more direct way to get to Bridger than the one we're traveling, that's the reason Battles kept trying to argue you out of starting the drive early.'

'He kept saying it was the weather he was worried about,' Earl Bates agreed, 'but I knew it wasn't. You're saying that now he won't bother to start his herd north?'

'He can't,' Trinity said. 'Not if you're at Bridger first with a healthy herd.' Trinity paused 'That's the reason I came after you, Bates; there's only one thing that Vincent Battles can do now to save the game: he's going to have to take your herd from you.'

'He'll play hell doing that!' Bates exploded.

'Will he? How many riders do you have?'

'Seven — you know that. Barely

enough to handle a herd *this* size.'

'That's what I mean. Battles has twice the number of men you have, and there's no need for him to leave any of them behind to tend the infected herd. He's given up on them. He'll try to catch up with you and set an ambush along the trail, knowing your men have their hands full already.'

'He'll never take this herd, not without killing me first,' Earl said.

'I think that's what he has in mind,' Trinity said quietly. 'He can't let you live, can he? Not you, Russell, nor . . . ' He broke off, for now he could see Holly, riding her little paint pony, drifting back along the flank of the herd. She had spotted them speaking together and must have wondered what was up. Bates lifted his eyes at her approach.

'Her, too,' Earl said somberly. 'Yes, I believe he would.'

'You've got to send outriders out to watch for him,' Trinity said.

'We've already discussed that, Lieutenant. This isn't the army out riding patrol.

I've barely got enough men to handle the herd. These cattle are hardly trail-broken yet, you know. I'm giving them a short day today, starting as late as we did, but they're still in a balky mood, wanting to break out of the herd and head back toward home range.'

'I know that,' Trinity answered with something like despair, 'but something must be done.'

'If you think so,' Earl Bates responded loudly, 'get out there yourself and look around — you're sure not doing any good here.'

The last part of that sentence, bellowed in his adopted Texas drawl, was the only portion of her brother's words that Holly heard. Bates winked at Trinity and said in a near-whisper, 'Do your best, Lieutenant. We could use any help you've got to offer right now.'

Holly watched in surprise as Trinity wheeled the bay horse at her approach and headed for the timber lining the valley. He did not wave to her or say a word, he simply obeyed Earl. Angrily,

Holly rode up beside her brother.

'Why did you do that, Earl? Run him off?' she asked, watching Trinity go.

'It just seemed like the thing to do,' Earl grumbled not wanting to frighten his sister. Because if what Trinity had told him was true — and it must be — Vincent Battles had also marked Holly for death.

Holly stared at her brother without comprehension, then just shook her head and rode stiffly back toward the point of the slow-moving herd.

★   ★   ★

The trees, mostly scrub pines with here and there a blue spruce, grew more numerous and now formed a narrowing corridor through which the herd must pass. The land on either side of the valley was thrust up, not ruggedly steep, but several hundred feet higher than the valley floor below. Trinity made his cautious way toward the ridge above, guiding the steady bay horse through

163

the pines. Willie Meese's rifle rode across his saddle bow.

'Do your best,' was what Earl Bates had urged him to do, and what he intended to do. Yet what hope was there for him against a dozen or more men? He briefly let himself, unrealistically, believe that Vincent Battles may have given up, seeing that his original plan was unworkable, and taken his men and ridden away, but Trinity knew that a man like Battles would not even consider such a course.

He would fight.

Atop the hill rise, Trinity tried to find a spot where he could look back along the valley. The trees, scattered though they were, obscured his line of sight. Looking to the east, away from the wind, he could see sunlight glinting on the face of the river Trinity had known was there but had never seen. It meandered its southerly way toward Texas. Undoubtedly Earl meant to drive the herd along it until it met the North Platte River, which had to be its source, to ensure that his cattle had water all along the route.

Somewhere along the river tonight, the cattle would be bedded down. Earl had said he meant them to have a short day, so it would not be long before his men began to bunch them for evening. The men themselves would be dog-tired. Keeping irritable cattle moving in a straight line when they were unused to life on the trail, was hard work. Watching the silver river flow, it occurred to Trinity that if he had conjectured all of this, so would Vincent Battles. And the best time to strike was on this first night with uneasy cattle and weary men wanting only to eat and then sleep. Trinity started his horse toward the river.

He had to talk to Earl Bates again, convince him that he needed to keep a few men up to watch for Vincent Battles. He knew the answer he would receive. The few men he had with him would already have to divide their sleeping time so that half of the cowboys could ride night herd, keeping watch over the restless herd. He couldn't have his men falling asleep in the saddle the next day if they had to pull a full night duty standing watch.

There had to be a way — perhaps he could convince a few men to grudgingly volunteer to ride guard. Because Vincent Battles would come to raid the herd on this night.

Trinity was convinced of it.

He made his way along the ridge, moving through the soft, cold shadows of the pines. From time to time, he paused and looked back, searching the hills, the long valley for approaching riders, but he was convinced they would not come until full darkness had fallen. There was nothing to be done just then but to follow the herd along toward the river where Earl meant to bed them down for an uneasy night.

He came upon their camp at sundown. The cattle lined along the river drank their fill looking around restlessly as if they liked none of this trail life. Weary cowboys kept them hemmed in along the river banks. There were constant attempts to break from the herd and the cow hands, on their cutting horses, were kept busy hieing the rebels back into the herd even now as dusk settled.

The sky was deep purple, with crimson etched against the few high clouds that remained from the passing storm. Trinity walked his bay around the camp, where men were already unrolling their bedding. There was no chuck wagon — apparently Earl had based this decision on the need for speed over the men's comfort. Cooky had not been invited along and so the men made catch as catch can meals of salt biscuits, jerky, whatever else they had managed to bring along. This could have been cause for rebelliousness, but apparently these men were used to hardship and loyal to Earl Bates. They comforted themselves with Earl's promise of a big payday ahead. Small cones of fire flared up, dotting the meadow.

These would have to be extinguished soon as complete darkness fell — one more discomfort the trail-weary men would endure, probably with much grumbling.

Trinity led the bay to water upstream from the cattle and stood watching the river, purple silk in this light, flow past. Beyond the river a chalky white bluff, studded with stately ponderosa pines stood, the last reddish glow of day reflected dully on its face. She slipped up beside him without him hearing her.

'Well, Lieutenant,' Holly said at his elbow, 'I thought my brother had driven you off.'

'I can't go,' Trinity said, turning to face her. All pretense now discarded, he added, 'It's in the army's best interest to see that this herd gets through to Bridger.'

'Is that why you're trying to help?' she asked, with a touch of coyness utterly at odds with her usual brusque manner.

'That's it,' he said, studying her

slightly parted, slightly amused lips.

'I thought maybe you wanted to aid the Owl,' Holly said.

'There's that, too,' he admitted. 'The two aren't exclusive motives. Rather they are intertwined.'

'If you are so willing to help, why haven't I seen you all afternoon? We could have used some help with the breakouts. Earl estimates we've already lost a dozen head. Fortunately, my brother, whatever else he is, is a cattleman — we started the drive with fifty more steers than we have promised to deliver.'

'Earl seems to know what he's doing,' Trinity replied, evading the question she had asked. How was he to answer her? That he suspected Vincent Battles and his men would ride down on them, if not this very night, soon, and one of Battles's aims was to eliminate the legitimate owners of the herd so that he could claim possession of the army beef?

'Well,' Holly said, with a sudden

surge of her more typical anger, 'if you won't tell a woman what's going on, would you please at least explain matters to Russell — he trusts you, you know.'

'Still?'

'What do you mean?'

'Now that he knows I'm an army officer — he is AWOL, you realize.'

Holly waved a fluttering hand in the air. 'For now that's the least of his concerns. He is only determined to get through to Fort Bridger with the cattle. It is a debt he owes to our father.'

'I'll talk to Russell,' Trinity said. He knew the little red-haired girl was miffed with him, but was not entirely sure why.

'This is my herd, you know!' Holly said sharply. 'No one else's. I have the right to know what's happening — even if I wear a divided riding skirt and not a pair of blue jeans.'

'It's not like that, Holly — ' Trinity said haltingly, but it was too late. She turned and stalked away before he could finish. The light was not good enough to see the flash in her golden eyes, but he was sure it was there. Someone needed to tame that girl's emotions down a little, he considered, and then, angry with himself, he stepped toward the bay, loosened its cinch to make it more comfortable and led it back toward the dying camp-fires and sleeping men. Russell Bates found Trinity first.

'Well?' Russell said with a hint of truculence as Trinity slipped the saddle from the bay preparatory to staking it out on the long grass. Trinity glanced at the shadowy man beside him. He could not see the angry fear on Russell's face, but he could sense it and detect it in the shaky resonance of his voice.

'Well what? Is everyone going to start a conversation with a demand?'

'I'm not demanding anything,' Russell countered. 'I just need some clarification. What in hell is going on, and what comes next?'

'I can't predict what comes next. I'm no seer.'

171

'You know what I mean,' Russell insisted.

'Maybe.' Trinity looked toward the settling camp. 'Let's move away a little, and I'll answer your questions.'

Russell hesitated, studying the dying camp-fires, the few men still sitting up, sipping coffee, talking in low voices, and nodded his head toward the forest verge. 'All right. Over there.'

When they had distanced themselves from the camp and stood isolated by the shadows of the night trees', Russell again asked his question, not much less sharply than before. 'Well? Trinity, you owe me an explanation.'

Trinity leaned his back against a pine and answered, 'I was sent down here for a reason, Russell. Men who had been fired from the Owl by Vincent Battles told someone that you were trying to sell infected beef to the army.'

'That's not — ' Russell objected automatically.

'Yes, it is,' Trinity had to tell him. He went on to repeat the story of his discovery of the second herd hidden in Bear Valley. 'Those were the cattle Battles meant to deliver.'

'It would have ruined the Owl!' Russell was stunned angry. 'When I tell Earl . . . '

'He already knows,' Trinity said.

'You never told me you were an army officer,' Russell complained.

'Would you have let me tag along if I'd told you that? Would you have trusted me?'

'I suppose not,' Russell said grudgingly. 'I would have suspected it was me you were after.'

'Yes — none of that is my business, although when we get to Bridger, I mean to put in a word for you. After all, it's not desertion yet, it's still the fairly minor infraction of AWOL.'

'It won't do any good — Captain Nunn has it in for me.'

'He's the post commander?'

'Acting commander. Colonel Little took a month's leave last month to visit his family in the East.'

'And you asked Nunn for a compassionate leave?'

'I told him my father was dying, yes. He refused to grant me leave.'

'That doesn't seem right,' Trinity said, frowning in the darkness. 'Tell me, what was Captain Nunn's position before he assumed command?'

'He did a little of everything,' Russell said. 'He was a line officer if there were hostilities; when things were calm he was a delegate to the Indian tribes. He was also procurement officer. Several other jobs —'

'Procurement officer,' Trinity said, interrupting. 'Then Lieutenant Ross, the man who inspected the herd, must have reported to Nunn.'

'I suppose so. Do you think Nunn is involved in all this — that that is why he didn't want me coming down to the Owl?'

'I don't know,' Trinity had to say. 'A lot of things could be. We'll find out eventually, and when I get back to division headquarters, Nunn may find himself in a lot of hot water.' For all Trinity knew that was one reason he had been sent to investigate — maybe Nunn had pulled some other shady deals in his time. His orders had not outlined the reasons behind the investigation, but simply ordered Trinity to conduct one. He had done his part; it was up to others with higher rank to figure out what to do next.

As if it had only now occurred to Russell, he said, 'If we beat Battles to Bridger — and we will — he's lost his game. Unless . . . '

'Yes, unless he strikes. And he can't have one of the Owl owners left alive to tell the story — that includes you.'

'You're right, of course,' Russell said, his voice now softening apologetically. 'I'm sorry, Trinity. I'm so stupid; I didn't have any idea what was going on.'

'Your father could have told you — Dalton Remy must have discovered the plan.'

'So they hanged him!'

'You saw him yourself. Why else would that have been done? I also believe that your father must have left you a letter explaining matters which you could not find because it had been destroyed before you got home.'

'Makes sense, doesn't it?' Russell said. 'Vincent Battles was already living in the house when we got there. He could have found it. Or . . . ' His voice trailed off. Trinity knew what he was going to say. Or one of his sisters did not want it found.

Not Holly, certainly. She was riding for the Owl brand, always would. She knew what the cattle sale meant to their future prospects — a large part of what was keeping her so on edge these days. As for Millicent, whose silk-clad arm Trinity had seen drawing Battles into her room that night, perhaps she had positioned herself where she figured she could not lose either way.

Trinity did not say this to Russell. The kid was clever enough to figure it out himself. Besides, the conclusion could prove to be wrong; it was based on no more than conjecture, and a single episode of contact between Millicent and Battles, which could have also been taken wrong by Trinity.

'He'll want to stop us soon,' Russell said, his thoughts far away from Trinity's own.

'Yes. It's a good bet that he'll make his try this very night,' Trinity agreed.

'What are we going to do?' the kid asked, now shaken.

'You're a soldier, Russell, as am I — we prepare for battle as well as we can, then wait for the enemy to make his move.'

10

It was a cold, moonless night. The wind had risen and it rattled its way through the pines where Trinity was standing watch. A chill had worked into his bones as midnight came and went. The river continued to slink past, black and sinuous. Now and then a cow bawled or a night rider rode past whistling or singing softly to calm the cattle, but for the most part the frigid night was still. Trinity's bay horse dozed, but Trinity could not allow himself that luxury. He knew that Vincent Battles and his men were out and about on this night even though he had not caught a sign of movement, heard a whisper of sound that did not belong.

Russell Bates stood his post not fifty yards from where Trinity had picked his own hill ridge position. Russell was motionless in the night, squatting on his heels, rifle across his knees. The kid had taken everything Trinity had to say quite seriously and so he suffered through the night as well. He was still an army man, and more important to him was the knowledge that the Owl was lost if Vincent Battles took this herd — that he, Earl, Holly would be shown no mercy if they tried to block his way. Again, without having mentioned it, Russell had placed his trust in Trinity.

The trouble was Lieutenant Trinity Ray Tucker had little to offer in the way of assistance or even advice. Battles had not arrived with his gunfighters — Trinity's first surprise of the night. He had been sure that Battles would strike early and hard. Someone among them must have been sent out as a scout, and the low, still-burning fires would have given the camp away. Yet Trinity had not seen, nor heard, anything of a prowling man.

Yet, he knew he could be wrong. Once on the plains, they had seen and heard nothing of a young Comanche who had scouted and then infiltrated

179

their camp, finding a pint of whiskey in a cavalryman's gear. Although they had guards posted, they had known nothing of the Indian until they found him among them in the morning, holding his drunken head in his hands.

No, there were men who were highly skilled at infiltration, and not all of them were Red men. Some among Vincent Battle's group were surely Civil War veterans, and could have even once been Confederate spies. A man learns many skills in life — if he lives long enough. And if he lives long, he is very good at his craft indeed.

A twig cracked behind Trinity and he looked that way, hands gripped on his rifle. It could have been a falling branch, brought down by the wind, or perhaps one trodden on by a deer in the forest. Trinity moved very slowly, shifting his position without rising to his feet. There was no way to signal Russell. Trinity stared at the darkness for long minutes, afraid to blink. Nothing moved, no shadow separated itself from the general gloom of night. No one was there — not this time.

He fought off sleep and tried to ignore the cold embrace of the night. He shivered and cursed silently the whole night through. Dawn came so slowly, unexpectedly, that Trinity thought he was imagining it at first. It had been that long since he had seen daylight, or so it seemed. A thin band of gold showed through the ponderosa pines atop the white bluff across the river; the rest of the eastern horizon was deep blue-violet. Below him Trinity could see some movement in the camp as the cowboys rose to face another exhausting day. Trinity got to his feet, stretched cold muscles and looked toward Russell, to see how he was doing.

Suddenly twenty of Battles' riders burst from the forest behind him and rode furiously down the slope. They seemed not to have seen Trinity. He went to a knee and shot at one of them, lifting the raider from his saddle. That brought a flurry of answering shots as

Trinity dove for the shelter of a fallen log, but no one pursued him. The focus of the Battles riders was on the herd below and the men there who now fled, dove for their weapons or stood frozen with shock as the riders bore down on them.

Then the firing on both sides escalated. The Owl men shot back with random intensity. Trinity saw another rider go down, saw a cowboy get to his feet, holding his chest to stagger away toward the river.

The cattle awoke as one mammoth beast. Panicked, they milled hesitantly, not knowing which way to run. They shied away from the onrushing riders, but could not turn and cross the river where escape was blocked by the white bluff. Earl Bates had employed his own stratagem — his night riders all were deployed to the south of the herd, blocking the cattle from returning to home range. That left the herd with only one way to run — to the north, nearer to Fort Bridger, which outside of those few scattered and lost, would only be an advantage to Owl when the steers had to be gathered once more.

Trinity recognized all of this without giving it examination. He had one job right now, and it was to try to drive the Battles gang off before . . . before someone could be hurt. He forked the bay and drove down on the raiders, rifle to his shoulder. He fired twice, saw one man go down, missed on the second shot, heard another rifle crack beside him. Russell Bates, his face grim, was also shooting on the run, his Winchester speaking as he charged down the slope toward the confused herd and bewildered chaos of the Owl riders.

From the south now, in a charge that would have done an army tactician proud, Earl Bates entered the fray leading his four night riders in a full charge toward the Battles men. One of the raiders span his horse, twisted in his saddle, in obvious confusion. The herd and the river were in front of him, Earl Bates charging from the south. He stiffened with shock as he realized now that there were guns behind him as well. He seemed to be looking directly at Russell Bates when the kid fired his rifle. The hired gun's hands flew up, he lost his grip on his rifle and toppled from the saddle as his horse made a mad dash northward. Trinity recognized the man. Dave Plimford would never trouble anyone again.

Trinity saw a horseman try to ride an Owl cowboy down as he lay in his bed, but the Owl rider had teeth. He rolled aside slightly as the man's horse jumped over and emptied three shots from his pistol into the animal's belly. The horse folded up and rolled, head first. The rider never got up — his neck was broken in the fall.

Two Owl hands had moved behind a row of milling cattle and they fired from behind the thousands of pounds of bulwark, taking down two men that Trinity saw. Sheltering behind confused cattle was a dangerous maneuver, but it had certainly saved their lives.

The dawn hour was a deadly riot of noise and motion. Trinity had lost count of the number of men he had seen go down before the sights of another man. He only knew that surprisingly the Owl men were standing up well under the attack. Perhaps, he thought, it was because nearly all of them had been on foot when the attack began. Their sights were steadier, their shots truer. Making his way toward the river, Trinity felt a near bullet tug the side of his shirt in its close passing — the same side Willie Meese had tagged him in. He spun, saw the rider bearing down on him and fired. The lead sent spinning from Trinity's rifle took the man high on the chest and he fell to the grass. Trinity did not think it was a killing shot, but he wasn't going to waste time checking on his enemy's wound. Not now. He needed to find . . .

The woman's shrill scream sounded clearly, rising above the clamor of gunfire and running animals. Trinity clamped his teeth together in anger and ran toward the river, moving as quickly as he could through the mass of cattle which had begun to surge northward. Heated bodies brushed past him, and horns as deadly as any weapon came within inches of his flesh. Weaving his way through the threatening herd, he reached the river in time to see Vincent Battles standing over Holly Bates. Holly held a pistol, but she let it dangle from her fingers as if the Colt were too heavy to lift.

Battles was hatless, his dark hair screening his eyes. His gun was leveled at Holly. Trinity heard the man say something, but he did not catch the words. Bracing himself, Trinity shouted out: 'Battles!'

The man's face was savagely twisted when he turned it toward Trinity. He shifted his sights to Trinity and pulled the trigger on his pistol. Trinity had not hesitated; he had fired first and his shot took Vincent Battles in the heart as Battles's own pistol's shot whined past and thudded into the flank of an unfortunate steer. Simultaneous with his own shot, Trinity had heard the report of still another gun. As he looked toward Holly, he could see that she had fired her own weapon. Smoke still trickled from her revolver's barrel as she lowered it. So which shot had done the trick? Who had saved whose life? Trinity had no wish to claim bragging rights about killing a man — there had been no choice, that was all — but he had the idea that Holly might find it easier on her conscience later if he were to take the responsibility.

But not now. For now he rushed to her and placed his rifle aside, going to his own knees to hold the trembling girl close to him, as the new sunlight sparkled on the face of the slowly flowing river beside them.

★   ★   ★

All things considered, the battle had been entered and won. It was not the sort of fight where their attackers would be expected to follow after them and continue to raid the herd, although Earl was aware of that possibility. With their leader dead, the others would likely see no point in continuing with Vincent Battles's plan. They would scatter and roam and become someone else's problem. Probably the law's.

The day broke cool and sunny. The confused herd had strung out along the river. Probably they would tire soon and could be gathered again without a great deal of difficulty. Which was good, for there were a number of wounded men riding herd now. Most of them could still sit their saddles, but one Owl rider had to be transported on a hastily constructed travois. And there were two dead left behind. They did not bother to search for dead or wounded raiders. That might seem cold, but these men had ridden in with cold intentions and ridden off with what they deserved.

Little had changed as the herd slowly gathered and again started north

— except that Holly now chose to ride next to Trinity. At times they would talk of nothing; at other times they rode long miles without sharing a word. Still when Trinity glanced at her, he would find those golden eyes fixed on him. It was vaguely comforting to know that she was beside him.

They spent the next night camped along the river, and by the following noon found themselves on the dry grass plains surrounding Fort Bridger. A troop of soldiers rode out to meet them, and the cattle were driven into the already constructed pens to bawl and mill and await their misfortune.

Trinity rode to report to the commander of the fort. He was relieved to find that Colonel Little — a pink, cheerful man — had returned from his vacation, and that the meeting with the procurement officer, Captain Nunn could be postponed. Earl and Holly arrived before Trinity had a chance to report, eager to conclude their own business with the army. The cattle had been counted and settled in; troopers now stood watch around the pens in case of a breakout while the Owl cowboys rested, slept or scoured the sutler's store for beer. The wounded were in the hands of the post surgeon.

Colonel Little was polite to Earl, effusively courteous to Holly. Russell, standing by but well away from the colonel's desk was ignored for the time being. The first sergeant who was also the purser, entered at the colonel's summons and opened the safe. A glowering, heavy man with suspicious eyes, he counted out the money and countersigned Colonel Little's signature of the disbursement slips without speaking a word. All of this seemed to be lost on Holly and on Earl Bates who recounted the money and handed it to his sister. Later it would be divided, a share to each of the four heirs with the cowhands payments to be drawn from each. The cattle would not have arrived without the work of the Texas cowhands, and each owed a share to them despite the fact that they were Earl's picked men.

Holly sensed before Earl did that it was time to leave, that Trinity and Russell had army business to discuss with the colonel. Her concerned eyes focused on Trinity for a while as she got to her feet, flickered to her brother and then fell away as she and Earl went out.

The glare of the afternoon sun was yellow-bright on the window behind the colonel who had lighted a cigar, taken a puff or two of it and now asked Trinity, 'You have a report for me, I expect.'

'Yes, sir,' Trinity said. 'It is a little lengthy and may prove somewhat distasteful.' The colonel's white eyebrows drew together as Trinity continued. 'A part of this involves your procurement officer, Captain Nunn. Is he to be found?'

'Nunn?' Colonel Little repeated, obviously confused. 'No, he should now be out on the reservation, letting the Indians know that their beef allotment has arrived. Why do you ask about Nunn?'

Trinity leaned forward, arms crossed

on his knee and began telling the long story. He finished with, 'There is no proof, of course, but it is possible that Captain Nunn conspired with Vincent Battles to have the army purchase the infected herd. It was clearly inedible, and would have proven to be a great insult to the Indians were it given to them.'

'Nunn?' the colonel said, looking at Trinity blankly. 'I won't believe it!'

'As I have said, there is no proof of it, Battles now being dead, but I ask you to consider that Nunn refused to grant Russell Bates compassionate leave, even knowing that his father was dying. Why? When he knew that the Owl was to be the provider of the army beef and that Russell could be usefully employed to bring the herd to Bridger, there only being his two sisters to manage the drive in his absence. Compassion and expedience both would have favored letting Bates return to his father's ranch.'

'He refused you?' the colonel said,

looking directly at Russell for the first time. The pink-faced officer was scowling now. 'I'll have to inquire into that, look at his records.'

'If any,' Trinity said a little sharply, forgetting his rank and position briefly.

'Your point has been made, Lieutenant,' Little said gruffly. 'I said I shall look into the matter.' Flicking ash from his cigar, he again fixed his pale gaze on Russell Bates. 'None of this absolves you from culpability,' he told Russell. 'The army can't let its soldiers make these decisions on their own. What kind of army would we be, then? You will have to stand some punishment.'

'Understood, sir,' Russell said, his face expressing disappointment and shame at once.

Trinity took a few moments to gather his thoughts, then said: 'Colonel, it is my understanding that Bates's term of enlistment is to end in a matter of months — six, I think. After he has served his punishment, could he not be considered for a hardship discharge?

There still remains no one else to manage the Owl ranch. His brother is bound for Texas once more. And the Owl, to again mention compassion and expedience, is the largest ranch nearby and certainly a source of future beef supplies — if . . . cordial relations are established and maintained.'

The colonel pushed his lower lip in and out, considering. He knew that Trinity had a point, but he was determined not to appear weak, it seemed. 'It is something to be considered,' he commented in the end. 'For now, Trooper Bates, I must ask you to surrender your weapons and allow yourself to be escorted to the stockade.'

It was the best, the only outcome they could have expected.

Holly was outside on the parade ground when the two burly soldiers, one on each elbow, escorted Russell to the stockade. Russell glanced at her once, shrugged, and let himself be taken away.

'How long will he be there, locked

up, I mean?' she asked Trinity as he met her there in the dusty hard-packed yard.

'I don't know. It's up to the colonel. It might not be a bad idea if you were to pay him a visit tomorrow to tell him how much you need Russell on the Owl now.'

'Womanly wiles?' Holly snorted. Her eyes were still troubled.

'The concern of an orphaned sister,' he replied.

'I suppose it's the least I can do,' Holly said as he escorted her toward the visitors' quarters, where both she and Earl had been assigned rooms for the night. She stopped abruptly before they reached the awning-shaded porch of the building. Four cavalrymen were walking their horses past and lavished Holly with appreciative glances. She was apparently unaware of them.

'What about you, Trinity? What are you going to do?'

'Do?' Trinity frowned, not understanding. 'Why I'm going to put on a blue suit and return to division headquarters for my next assignment.'

'Why?' Holly asked, stepping nearer, her body only inches from his.

'What do you mean, 'why'. I have a lot of time in the army, a pension waiting for me when I'm through, free meals, free medical care — all of the fringe benefits.'

'Not all of them,' Holly said, her eyes and voice more coquettish than ever before.

'What are you talking about?' Trinity asked, already knowing what she meant.

'You could come back to the Owl with us, take over the foreman's job — we have none now. Trinity, it's my understanding that an officer can resign his commission. Am I wrong?'

'No,' he said honestly. 'But it takes more than just announcing it, straddling a pony and riding off. If I did something like that, I'd be in as much trouble as Russell has gotten into — more.'

'How long would it take . . . if you decided to do something like that?' Holly asked, and those golden eyes of hers were on his now, her fingers toying with the buttons on his shirt front.

'I don't know,' he said, taking a step away from her. 'I've never considered it.'

'You could find out,' she persisted.

'I could — just so I'd know if it ever comes up someday,' Trinity said. The sun felt intolerably hot; the humming in his head was as if he had a swarm of bees in his hat. 'For now I have to get over to the base officers' quarters to make sure I have a bed for the night.'

He spoke in a rush like a confused schoolboy. Spinning away, he strode across the parade ground, nearly walking in front of a trio of mounted soldiers. With his cheeks glowing red, he turned for one last look at Holly and saw her standing in the doorway watching. Beside her stood Earl Bates with a knowing smile on his broad face. It struck Trinity as a pleased, yet somehow pitying look.

11

There were formalities to be taken care of. On that evening, Captain Nunn returned from the tribal lands and was immediately summoned to the colonel's office. Nunn professed his innocence strongly, protesting that anyone who would suggest he would accept a bribe for purchasing unhealthy cattle was a damned liar. In the morning, they found him gone. A patrol was sent in pursuit, but he had a good lead, and in that rough country it was doubtful that they would ever find the man.

'Nunn must have thought that Vincent Battles was still alive and willing to testify against him,' Trinity commented as he met Holly at the sutler's store. It was early in the day and the soldiers, out on duty, had left the place virtually deserted. 'I'm given to understand that that was the tactic Colonel Little used.'

Holly wore a pink dress with a tiny red ribbon on the bodice. It had been purchased the evening before in the store. She saw Trinity studying it. 'I got it at a bargain,' she protested although he was not going to comment on the price — it was not his business, after all. 'The wife of one of the officers ordered it months ago, but when it got here she decided that the color wasn't right for her.'

'Fine,' was all Trinity said. 'So I guess Nunn has paid, or will pay for his involvement with Vincent Battles. The business is finished.'

'Hmm,' Holly said as if only marginally interested. 'Have you considered the other matters we still have to deal with?' She lowered herself on to a wooden bench beside the sutler's door, fanning her skirts out.

'Such as . . . ?'

'The infected herd, of course,' Holly said almost accusingly. 'We can't continue to have them using our grass. And there's always the worry that one of our roaming steers along the Dos Picos might mingle with them and bring the fever back to the Owl.'

'Yes. They have to be gotten rid of,' Trinity agreed.

'How, Trinity? We can't sell them off to some unsuspecting party. We can't let them go free on the range.'

'No, you can't,' he said, carefully ignoring the use of the plural pronoun Holly had employed.

'You know, Holly,' Trinity said, settling on the bench beside her. 'Years ago, before there were railheads and cattle towns like Wichita and Abilene, there was no market for the thousands of cattle in the Texas lands. Men were spoken of as being cattle rich and cash poor. During the years of the Civil War, when most of the men were off to war, the cattle, unmanaged, had multiplied wildly.'

'I don't need a history lesson,' Holly said a little tartly.

'I know — you're only worried about your own problem,' Trinity said patiently. 'Listen to me a minute, will you? What was done in those times to try to eke out a living on the land was to use the cattle for hides and tallow alone. These were transported to seaports like Galveston and sold there.'

'Trinity . . . ' Holly said with some exasperation. Across the way a troop of cavalrymen was performing a mounted drill.

'I'm trying to tell you, Holly, that the tainted cattle herd might be used for tallow and hides. We need to only find some fellows who are broke and hard up for work and hand over the herd. There's no profit in it for you, of course, but then they weren't yours to begin with. It would keep the fever from spreading accidentally, and keep those poor creatures from living for nothing and of dying one by one of the sickness.'

'Can it be done?' she asked, suddenly interested.

'I'm sure it can — in the old days they had no trouble finding men to go out on the plains to work as buffalo skinners. I'll ask the colonel and some of the other men — someone will know of local people who need the money badly enough to take on the job.'

'Well, if it can be done — that seems to be the way to go about it. Otherwise, we just have a sickly herd dying over on the Bear Valley range with nothing anyone can do for them or with them. It's the best of the lot of poor options, I suppose.'

'I think so.'

'Trinity?' She turned those golden eyes on him. 'What about the rest of the business we still have to take care of?'

* * *

It was ten days before they opened the heavy door to the cell where Russell Bates had been spending his days of punishment. His jailers led him to the front door of the squat, heavy-walled building and let him go out into the sunshine which was so brilliant after ten days of near-darkness that it hurt his eyes and sent a shock through his brain.

He slitted his eyelids and remained for a while in the scant shade of the awning. He felt disoriented. It was as if he had never before been on the army post. Where was he to go now? He had been given no instructions.

Blinking into the sun glare he saw two familiar but unlikely appearing figures striding across the hard-packed earth of the parade ground to meet him. The woman, dressed in a pink dress wearing a white straw hat looked like — had to be — Holly, but she looked so unlike her regular self that he could not at first be sure.

The tall man beside her wore dark trousers, a white shirt and pearl-gray Stetson. Their arms, Russell noticed, were linked.

'Hi, Russ!' Holly called out. Her voice was familiar, yet somehow different, softer.

'You waited for me?' Russell asked in wonder.

'Sure — it was only ten days, after all.'

'But someone should be taking care of the Owl,' Russell protested.

'Earl started that way days ago. He's going to watch things until we get back.'

'Until you get back,' Russell said glumly. 'I've still got six months duty, in case you've forgotten.'

'I haven't forgotten,' Holly said cheerfully. 'Colonel Little has agreed to give you a hardship discharge, Russ. You're free to ride with us.' Russell was obviously stunned. When he spoke it was with a trembling voice, as he tried to digest this fact.

'I didn't expect to see you, Trinity,' he finally managed to say. 'Still not in uniform?'

'He's resigned his commission,' Holly said, clutching Trinity's arm more tightly as she looked up at him. 'He'll be riding back to Owl with us — as our new foreman.'

'How . . . ' It was too much for Russell to take in all at once. 'You both waited for me?' It dawned on him as he saw the glint of sunlight on the golden ring Holly wore on her third finger. 'You're married!'

'We'd better be — now,' Holly said. He thought she blushed a little.

'The post chaplain did the job,' Trinity told Russell.

'Well, I'll be damned!' Russell said, shaking Trinity's hand. 'I hope you know how to tame a wildcat.' He glanced at his sister.

'She's settled down a little,' Trinity replied. 'Now that there's not so much trouble on her mind.'

'Well, fine. I wish you the best,' Russell said sincerely. He grinned suddenly. 'Let's get on the trail right away, if you don't mind. I've seen enough of this place, and I'm ready to go home.'

*   *   *

The three trailed into the Owl yard two days later, travel-weary and dusty. The skies held clear on this late afternoon and there was a cooling breeze blowing,

205

shifting the upper limbs of the cotton-wood trees and rustling the heavy boughs of the blue spruce. They approached the house from the rear and swung down there, tying their horses up thankfully. They had all had enough riding for a while. They did not see Earl or any of his Texas hands around. As they neared the porch outside the kitchen in a group, Cooky stepped out of the doorway, glancing back.

'Just exchanging recipes,' he said, although no one had asked him.

Alicia was humming to herself as they trooped in, closing the door behind them. Trinity and Holly glanced at each other, but said nothing, only greeting Alicia.

Passing through into the front room, they found Earl setting a fire in the fireplace. The big, blond rancher glanced up from his work.

'Is everything all right around here, Earl?' Holly asked, half-expecting bad news the way things had gone in her life lately. Her brother stood, dusting his hands on his jeans.

'Fine as can be,' Earl Bates told her. 'We moved the herd a little farther down the valley to new grass. My men have been paid off and they're mostly healthy or healed. I guess we'll be starting back to the home ranch in the morning. You can ask them if anyone wants to stay on the Owl, but I really need them all down home.'

'We don't want to strip you of your crew,' Trinity told him. 'It will take a while, but we'll find some good men — I'm thinking some of the old crew might want to drift back to the Owl with Vincent Battles gone.'

'Hope so,' Earl said. 'Holly, I need to talk to you, Millicent and Russell about settling accounts. I've already tapped my cut to pay my men. We need to run through the numbers and make sure everyone gets his fair share.'

'Where is Millicent?' Trinity wondered, looking around.

'She's been staying upstairs since I've been here, acting all sulky as if something had gone wrong.' Earl shook his head. He glanced at Trinity and said, 'Sometimes I wonder if . . . '

Then he shut up. Trinity thought he knew what Earl was going to say. He, too, must have wondered if it was possible that Millicent had thrown in her lot with Vincent Battles and had her plans upset when Battles's scheme fell apart.

'You told her what happened on the trail, then?' Holly inquired. 'That Battles was dead.'

'Yes, that was when she took to her room,' Earl said unhappily. 'Anyway, Holly, can we get financial business taken care of this evening? I've got a ranch in Texas that needs seeing to.'

After that the group split up — Earl to tell his crew that they were headed home, Russell to wash up and take a nap. Trinity and Holly sat on the old leather sofa in front of the slowly growing fire while beyond the window the sky purpled and the wind began to die down.

'I've got one matter I wanted to

discuss with you,' Trinity said, putting his arm over Holly's shoulders. She turned to him with a smile.

'We have to wait until everyone else has gone to bed,' she said with a laugh.

'Not that,' Trinity said with a grin of his own. 'It's a small matter to us, but important to someone else. I wonder if Tonio can't be put in charge of the horses full-time. He loves the animals and old Roger just isn't up to it anymore. Roger can be a sort of yard man around here, just raking and hoeing weeds — whatever needs to be done. I think he would be happier without any real responsibilities anyway.'

'Go ahead and do it,' Holly agreed. 'So long as it doesn't upset Roger. He's been with us for a very long time — he was one of the men who worked for my father when they drove the first cattle on to the Owl range.'

Trinity did not think the old man would mind if it was explained gently to him. From what he had seen of Roger, it must now be a strain for him even to throw a saddle over a horse's back. He did know that Tonio would be thrilled.

They settled in quiet, comfortable companionship as the day went to night and the fire burned low. Holly stretched, yawned and rubbed her shoulders. 'I'd better poke that fire to life,' she said. 'It's starting to get cool in here.'

Trinity watched her rise, walk to the fireplace, her slender figure both a memory and a promise in his mind. The sound of rustling garments behind him brought Trinity's head around. Millicent, in back crepe, stood at the bottom of the staircase. Her eyes were wide, dark in her pale face. There was a big Colt revolver in her hand.

'I know what you did,' she said, drawing nearer. 'You killed Vincent Battles.'

'Millicent . . . ' Trinity said, getting to his feet.

'You killed Vincent Battles, and now I am going to kill you.'

12

Millicent held the Colt revolver steady in both of her hands. Her dark eyes glinted crazily in the firelight. Trinity was certain that she meant to do what she had said. He was not wearing a gun, and even if he had been, he doubted he could have shot her. That left him with few options. He dove for the floor as the big gun's echo racketed through the room. Her shot came within inches of his head.

Holly had turned from the fireplace at her sister's voice. Now with a hiss, she flung the iron poker in her hand at Millicent. It windmilled through the space between them and struck Millicent on her neck and head. The woman dropped to the floor, losing her grip on the revolver. Millicent still did not move as Trinity rose and scrambled toward her. He tossed the pistol aside and checked Millicent's wounds.

'Well?' Holly asked.

'She'll make it. You just knocked her cold. Help me get her upstairs to her bed.'

'All right,' Holly said with resignation. 'I suppose it's only human to do that much for her.' Holly's eyes remained angry as they hoisted Millicent from the floor, carrying her by her shoulders and feet toward the stairs. 'Don't you remember, Trinity — I told you she could shoot.'

* * *

Breakfast was subdued. Russell, Trinity and Holly were the only ones at the table. Russell had been up to visit Millicent earlier and he told them, 'She's moaning and crying a lot. There's a lump on her skull. Otherwise, I think she's all right now. She's bound to figure out sooner or later that Vincent Battles never loved her, that he was just using her. Until then,' he shrugged, 'she's going to be a sad presence in this house.'

'When was she not?' Holly said sharply.

Alicia served them breakfast then. Steaming cornbread and omelets, Spanish style, with melted cheddar cheese and onions inside and a thick blanket of white *queso fresco* cheese over it, smothered with rich red salsa heavy with fresh green and red peppers and cilantro. Trinity hoisted his fork and glanced across the table at Holly who was already working on her omelet.

'I thought you didn't care for Alicia's omelets,' he said.

'Holly!' Russell Bates laughed. 'She'd have one every morning if she could.'

'But . . . ' Trinity said, 'That morning we first met out on the range — you said the reason you were out riding alone that early was because you couldn't stand the way Alicia fixed your eggs. Why did you tell me that, if it wasn't so? What were you doing riding alone out there, Holly? You can't have just been looking for . . . '

'Eat,' Holly said, her golden eyes smiling at him. 'Just eat, you big lug.'

We do hope that you have enjoyed reading this large print book.

Did you know that all of our titles are available for purchase?

We publish a wide range of high quality large print books including:
Romances, Mysteries, Classics
General Fiction
Non Fiction and Westerns

Special interest titles available in large print are:
The Little Oxford Dictionary
Music Book, Song Book
Hymn Book, Service Book

Also available from us courtesy of Oxford University Press:
Young Readers' Dictionary
(large print edition)
Young Readers' Thesaurus
(large print edition)

For further information or a free brochure, please contact us at:
Ulverscroft Large Print Books Ltd.,
The Green, Bradgate Road, Anstey,
Leicester, LE7 7FU, England.
Tel: (00 44) 0116 236 4325
Fax: (00 44) 0116 234 0205

DERAILED

Owen G. Irons

An outlaw gang has kidnapped the Colorado and Eastern train, leaving the passengers afoot in a winter blizzard. Tango and Ned Chambers, the men hired to prevent such things from happening, are left alone on the frozen prairie with a wealthy widow and a brother of the US vice-president. Now all they have to do is recover the train, get through to Denver and bring to justice those responsible for the outrage, without allowing harm to come to their charges . . .

FUGITIVE RUN

Chet Cunningham

David West is a fugitive on the run, despite his innocence. He leaves Boston and heads for Junction Springs, Colorado. Here he meets detective Susan Kramer, who needs him to help discover the identity of her father's killer. When, eventually, the killer is nailed and brought to trial, West returns to Boston with his new expertise determined to seek justice and catch the man who killed his fiancée. Can West avenge her death and once more find love?

SUNDOWN AT SINGING RIVER

Ty Kirwan

Gunfighter Jorje Katz rides into the town of Singing River to begin a new life. On arrival he discovers that the partner he had financed is long dead. With no money to his name, Jorje's only option is to become a hired gun in a war that is raging between two political factions in the town. Dragged back into his old ways, Jorje despairs — until he is appointed Sheriff. At last it seems that his dreams can finally be realised . . .

SILVER TRACK

Caleb Rand

Having travelled to a wild frontier town in search of answers about his brother's death, Ben Jody finds himself not only in the middle of a bitter conflict between rival railroad companies, but also accused by the Army of being a deserter. With his good name tarnished and the law hot on his heels, he has little choice but to run. On discovering who is responsible for his brother's death though, Ben decides to ride right into the face of danger . . .